Would she ever feel safe?

Anne's thoughts kept churning through the morass of danger that lurked. Would a hit man slit her throat as she slept? As she came out of the school building? Went to the grocery store?

And what of Professor Patrick McClain? And how much she enjoyed being around him?

Thinking about Patrick was more productive than worrying about the threat she couldn't control. There was something very steady and reassuring about him that drew her in and made her wish he could see her as she really was.

But she couldn't afford to get attached to anyone. She was pretty sure she could keep from revealing her past, but she wasn't sure that she could keep her lonely heart from wanting what she couldn't have.

A friend. Love. A life without fear.

Books by Terri Reed

Love Inspired Suspense

Strictly Confidential #21
*Double Deception #41
Beloved Enemy #44
*Her Christmas
    Protector* #79
*Double Jeopardy #109

Love Inspired

Love Comes Home #258
A Sheltering Love #302
A Sheltering Heart #362
A Time of Hope #370
*Giving Thanks
    for Baby* #420

*The McClains

TERRI REED

At an early age Terri Reed discovered the wonderful world of fiction and declared she would one day write a book. Now she is fulfilling that dream and enjoys writing for Steeple Hill Books. Her second book, *A Sheltering Love,* was a 2006 RITA® Award Finalist and a 2005 National Reader's Choice Award Finalist. Her book *Strictly Confidential,* book five of the Faith at the Crossroads continuity series, took third place in the 2007 American Christian Fiction Writers Book of the Year Award. She is an active member of both Romance Writers of America and American Christian Fiction Writers. She resides in the Pacific Northwest with her college-sweetheart husband, two wonderful children and an array of critters. When not writing, she enjoys spending time with her family and friends, gardening and playing with her dogs.

You can write to Terri at P.O. Box 19555, Portland, OR 97280, or visit her on the Web at www.loveinspiredauthors.com, or leave comments on her blog at http://ladiesofsuspense.blogspot.com/.

DOUBLE JEOPARDY

Terri Reed

Steeple Hill®

Published by Steeple Hill Books™

STEEPLE HILL BOOKS

Steeple
Hill®

ISBN-13: 978-0-373-44299-7
ISBN-10:   0-373-44299-8

DOUBLE JEOPARDY

www.SteepleHill.com

Printed in U.S.A.

And those who know your name put their trust in you; for you, O Lord, have not forsaken those who seek you.

—*Psalms* 9:10

To my children; you are my joy and my blessing.

PROLOGUE

March

Gunfire!

The plush private suite on the top floor of the Palisades Casino and Resort in downtown Atlantic City, New Jersey rocked with the deafening noise of gunfire, echoed by the screams of its once-privileged occupants.

The woman's heart slammed painfully against her ribs and a cry burst from her lungs. The tray of glasses she held fell to the carpeted floor with a thud, the liquor soaking the rug. The stench of alcohol mixed with the smell of gunpowder. A potent combination.

She dove behind the free-standing bar. Crouched and shuddering with terror, she clapped her hands over her ears to muffle the retort of weapons firing and the sounds of men dying.

"Oh, God in Heaven, please, help me," she prayed, rocking on her heels. She didn't know why she was

praying. Did God even exist? But if there was a time to glom on to any hope that He was real, now was that time.

A man's body dropped to the floor beside her. She gasped. Jean Luc Versailles, the owner of the Palisades, groaned. Thankfully he wasn't dead, but a deep crimson stain spread across the white dress shirt beneath his tuxedo jacket.

Adrenaline pumping, she grabbed him by the arm and struggled to drag him closer to the relative safety behind the bar. Tears clogged her throat and ran down her cheeks. He had always been nice to her.

"You have to get out of here," Jean Luc said with a croak, his voice expressing the pain reflected in his dark eyes.

"You're hurt," she said inanely, her mind trying to recall her first-aid training from high school P.E. Like that had prepared her to deal with a gunshot wound.

Pressure. She had to apply pressure to stop the bleeding. Gagging from the sight and smell of blood, she yanked two bar towels from the shelf beside her and pressed them to his shoulder. She cringed as more gunshots filled the air.

His hand fastened around her wrist like a vise. "My jacket pocket. Get my wallet."

Keeping one hand firmly on the towels, she slid out his black leather billfold from the inside pocket of his tailor-made jacket with her free hand.

"Now what?" she asked.

He closed her hand tightly around the billfold and

thrust it against her stomach. "Take the money. Use it. Disappear." He let go of her and pushed himself up to a seated position, the bar at his back. "Escape through the wall panel. Run and don't stop. Go."

Acutely aware of the massacre taking place on the other side of the bar, she whispered, "I can't leave you. We need the police."

"No police." He struggled to his knees, swayed slightly, and reached around her. From behind several liquor bottles he pulled out a large silver gun.

She shrank back, wishing she'd called in sick today. Wishing Jean Luc hadn't invited Raoul Domingo to his private suite. Wishing she were anywhere but here.

But wishing never did any good.

His dark gaze pierced her. "On three."

"What about you?"

He got a foot beneath him. "Just go. One. Two." He staggered to his feet, the gun raised in his shaky hand. "Three!"

Self-preservation, survival instinct, whatever, took over. She scrambled to her feet and in a half-crouch ran toward the mirrored wall.

The sight reflected there made her stumble. Her heart thumped in her chest. Anticipation wound a tight knot in her gut.

Any moment the blast of a bullet would slam into her. But she didn't want to die here today. Every muscle in her body, tightened in readiness, made movement painful.

She flung the potted fichus out of the way and pushed desperately at the edge of the mirrored wall.

A slight click and the wall opened. She squeezed through into Jean Luc's opulent private bedroom in the hotel. The blur of red satin and black leather assaulted her already heightened senses as she dashed for the door leading to the hall on this floor.

Cautiously she peered out.

The corridor was empty. Too afraid to wait for an elevator, she rushed to the stairwell and descended the stairs as rapidly as she could without flying face-first into the concrete walls. She hit the outside door with her whole body and stumbled into the hotel staff's section of the underground garage.

Through the sea of employee cars she saw no one, friend or foe. She raced toward where she parked, fumbling to get her key out of her pants pocket.

Her little blue hatchback was a welcome sight. With shaky hands, she unlocked the door, slid into the driver's seat and started the engine. The gears ground as she shifted into Reverse and almost simultaneously pressed on the gas.

The small car shot backward. She slammed on the brake and shifted into Drive. Her foot pounced on the gas and the car rocketed forward, the tires squealing as she zipped around the curved lot and jetted out onto the dark, deserted street. This late at night people were either at home asleep or inside one of the many casinos along the strip.

She drove, hardly paying attention to the direction

shc headed until she came to a screeching halt at a red light. Her breathing came shallow and fast. She checked the rearview mirror. As far as she could tell, no one had followed her.

Hopefully she'd had enough of a head start that she could stop somewhere and figure out what to do. Where to go. She needed to go to the police.

Because she'd witnessed murder.

Jean Luc had said no police. But Jean Luc was dead.

Her stomach roiled with terror.

Nothing she'd ever faced in her life had prepared her for this.

She pulled the car into the parking lot of a fast food joint. The bright fluorescent sign illuminated the inside of the car. She'd thrown Jean Luc's wallet on the passenger seat.

Now she picked up the supple leather and thumbed through the contents. Her eyes widened at the number of hundred- and thousand-dollar bills inside the wallet. She swallowed hard.

He'd planned on dying when he'd given her the money.

Heart aching at his sacrifice, she let loose with fresh tears. He'd been a kind and thoughtful employer.

He'd once said she reminded him of his little sister. She didn't know if that was true but she had liked him and admired him.

A pang pierced her heart.

He'd given his life to set her free.

And doomed her to a life of fear.

Did she dare take the time to go back to her loft apartment? Was there anything there worth grabbing? Thanks to Jean Luc, she had enough cash to start over anywhere she wanted.

Only…she couldn't forget the image she'd seen in the mirror seconds before she'd made her escape.

A gun firing at Jean Luc, his body crumpling to the floor.

The expression of hatred on the man holding the gun that delivered the fatal bullet would forever be seared on her brain.

A man she recognized.

The cold eyes of Raoul Domingo would haunt her nightmares.

Where could she hide that was far enough out of reach from New Jersey's most feared mob boss?

Lieutenant Lidia Taylor, Chief State Investigator for the Atlantic County Major Crimes Squad, walked out of the interrogation room with frustration pulsing in her veins. Yes, Jean Luc Versailles's Thai girlfriend, Nikki Song, confirmed that the casino owner had set up a meeting with Raoul Domingo for that night. But knowing about a meeting and proving Domingo was a murderer were two different things.

"Good work," General Investigator Section Detective Rick Grand, Lidia's partner, stated when he met her in the hall, his voice full of respect.

"It isn't enough. I've already got D.A. Porter breathing down my neck on this."

"I have two resort guests who will swear they saw Domingo and his gang get in the elevator," Rick replied.

More frustration kicked Lidia in the gut. "That still doesn't put him in the suite or the gun in his hand. We need to find that girl on the video." The hotel's security camera had shown a woman running out of the hotel employee entrance a few minutes after Versailles's death.

Rick smiled like a Cheshire cat sitting on the moon. "I have a lead on another person who might be able to put Domingo in the same room with Jean Luc."

Lidia stilled. "Details."

"Housekeeping had a maid scheduled to attend to Jean Luc's private room right about the time Domingo entered the elevator. The maid never returned to finish her shift."

"Who else knows about this?"

Rick shrugged. "Just you and me. And housekeeping."

Exhaling an adrenaline laced breath, Lidia said, "Find me that maid before Domingo does."

"Hey, Taylor," called the desk sergeant, Morales, from the end of the hall, his weathered face glowing with interest. "I've got a live one for you."

Lidia followed the heavyset officer to the public waiting room.

A long-haired blond woman sat in a hard plastic

chair near the vending machine. Her frightened blue gaze kept darting to the door as if either expecting someone to come in or as if she were contemplating running out.

"Can I help you?" Lidia asked as she stopped in front of the woman, blocking he exit.

Slowly the young woman stood. Blood splattered the front of her gold and black uniform. The same uniform worn by the hotel staff at the Palisades Casino. Anticipation hit Lidia like the business end of a Taser.

The woman spoke, her voice low and shaky. "My name in Anne Jones. I want to report a murder."

ONE

May

"Really, Patrick, this won't be as disruptive as you imagine. The new computers and software are very easy to navigate. They will just take a little getting used to."

Patrick McClain stared at the Web site for the fancy new system as Sharon Hastings, the Economics Department staff administrator, pointed to the computer monitor sitting on her desk.

Sharon was efficient and talented at her job, but whenever Patrick entered her domain of scattered files and stacks of papers, he had to wonder how she accomplished anything. The array of clutter made him itch.

Patrick twitched his shoulders beneath his tweed sport coat. "What's wrong with the computers we have now?"

In her mid-sixties with graying hair held in a loose

bun at her nape and rows of sparkly beaded necklaces hanging down her front, Sharon was a throwback to the seventies, despite her tech savvy. She sighed with a good dose of patience that always brought heat to Patrick's cheeks.

"The school received a grant to buy the new computers. We need to update and stay with the times," she stated calmly.

He understood, but that didn't mean he had to like the change. All of his work was on his computer. "This is going to be a nightmare."

Sharon's lined face spread into an understanding smile. "Don't worry. We have temps coming in to do the software integration. You won't have to do a thing until you have the new notebook computer in your hand. This will be very freeing and much more time-efficient, since you will be able to take your computer home with you and work there instead of coming on campus every weekend."

Taking a cloth from his sport coat's front pocket, he removed his glasses and cleaned the lenses. He thought about his apartment in Boston's Back Bay. His name was on the lease and he did sleep there occasionally, but he didn't consider the stark walls and stiff furniture home.

No, the house he grew up in was home.

But his mother had made it clear recently that she didn't want him coming "home" so often. She'd lamented that it was time for him to get a life. And for her to start living again.

Whatever that meant.

"Well, I just hope whomever you have working on this is competent," Patrick stated and replaced his glasses onto the bridge of his nose.

Sharon inclined her head. "I'm sure they will be." A knock sounded at the door of Sharon's office. "Come in," she called.

The door opened and a young woman, devoid of any hint of makeup, who looked to be in her early twenties, stepped inside. Her short burgundy-red hair spiked up in all directions and her big violet-colored eyes showed hesitance and wariness as she glanced at Patrick. She wore an ill-fitting dress suit and though the drab brown fabric hung off her shoulders, Patrick's gaze fell to the hem of her skirt where her shapely calves were emphasized by heeled pumps.

"I'm sorry, I don't mean to interrupt," the woman said in a soft voice.

"We were just finishing," Patrick offered, feeling the need to banish her uncertainty.

She smiled slightly, and the soft curving of her mouth unexpectedly grabbed at his chest. She turned her gaze to Sharon. "Mrs. Hastings?"

Sharon stood and came around the desk to offer her hand. "I am. And you are...?"

"Anne Johnson. The admin office sent me up."

"Ah, my temp. Did they explain the project to you?"

"Yes."

"Perfect. I was just telling Professor McClain about the new computer system."

A strange lump formed in Patrick's stomach. This young, fresh-faced student was not his idea of a competent person to handle such sensitive material.

He gave Sharon a sharp-eyed glance. If she noticed his disapproval she ignored it. Instead Sharon pretty much dismissed him by pulling Miss Johnson toward the computer to show off the new notebook-style system that would be arriving within the next few days.

The cell phone attached to his belt vibrated. He glanced at the caller ID. His sister. He needed to take the call, but he wanted to stay and learn more about this temp that would be working on the computer issue.

"I'll be going now," he said, unsuccessfully trying to hide his irritation at being ignored by the two ladies.

Sharon nodded distractedly. Patrick met Miss Johnson's wide-eyed stare for a moment before she hastily dropped her violet gaze. The impact of those interestingly colored eyes left him slightly off balance. He frowned some more. He didn't like being off balance.

He stepped out into the corridor and flipped open his phone. "Meggie?"

He listened to his sister's tear-filled tirade. Finally he interrupted, "Meg, have you talked to Dr. Miller about this? Hon, you know how the subway upsets you, so why do you insist on taking it?" He tried to keep the frustration from his voice, but couldn't quite manage it.

"No, I'm not upset with you. Things here are a bit...stressful."

He acknowledged her suggestion that he see a psychologist for stress management. "I'll take that into consideration. Promise me no more subway rides. Take a cab or walk. Isn't that one of the reasons you moved to Manhattan was so you could walk instead of sit in a car?

"I love you, too, sis."

He hung up with a sigh. As proud as he was of his little sister for forging out a life in the art world which she was passionate about, he couldn't help but worry. Her obsessive-compulsive disorder flare-ups seemed to be more frequent the more she tried to push herself to overcome the disorder. But at least she knew he'd always be here for her.

As he headed back down the hall of the fourth floor of the main building on the lower campus of Boston College, Patrick's thoughts turned back to the new computer system and he decided he'd *double* backup all of his work, just in case. He was *not* going to trust the wide-eyed Miss Johnson with his life's work.

Lidia entered the outer office of the District Attorney, Christopher Porter, in the old courthouse of Atlantic City. The wood paneled walls and wooden desk made the small space seem cramped. In the corner next to the filing cabinet, where a woman in a blue sweater and navy slacks sat with an open drawer in front of her, a limp palm tree tried to bring some color to the room.

The woman turned as Lidia noisily closed the door behind her.

"Lieutenant Taylor?"

Lidia nodded and flashed her badge at the mousy brown-haired woman. Her pale face and unrefined features were dominated by wide hazel eyes. The name plate on the desk read Jane Corbin.

"You may go in, he's expecting you," Jane said, her voice low and timid. She adjusted her sweater over her ample chest and turned back to the filing cabinet.

So much for chitchat. Lidia gave one solid knock on the wood door before entering. Porter sat at his desk, his gaze on a report in front of him. His salt and pepper hair caught the late afternoon sunlight streaming through the window behind him. He looked up and pinned her to the floor with his intense gray eyes. "Hello, Lieutenant. Have a seat."

Lidia sat across the scarred pine desk. Porter didn't waste time with pleasantries but went right to reviewing the details of Domingo's arrest.

Domingo's DNA matched the blood found at the crime scene. They had him on tape entering the hotel and exiting through a service door during the time of the murders. And they had an eyewitness. It couldn't get better than that.

For over two hours, Porter shot off questions and she shot right back with answers.

But no matter how much he pushed Lidia, he wouldn't find any flaw in the investigation or the arrest of Domingo. They'd done everything by the letter of the law. No way would Domingo walk on a technicality from the homicide division.

From this point on, the burden to convict lay with the D.A.'s office.

Tired and hungry, she finally barked, "Enough." If she didn't get out of the musty office she was going to scream.

Porter started, his sharp gray eyes widening slightly. He wasn't accustomed to her abrupt manner but in time, if they continued to work together, she had no doubt, he'd get used to her.

"All right. Fine. For now." He closed the file lying in front of him with a snap. "We have a solid case. As long as our witnesses continue to cooperate, we should see Domingo behind bars by summer's end."

"They'll cooperate," Lidia assured him with confidence. The three witnesses all claimed to have held Jean Luc Versailles in high regard. All three were reluctant to come forward but thankfully were doing the right thing.

"They're secure?"

Frustration twisted in her gut. "Two are in WITSEC. One refused, but is in hiding. We've maintained contact with all three."

"I'm pushing to have the case moved up on the docket. But you know the system."

"Yeah, like molasses in a freeze."

Porter gave her a sidelong glance as he closed and then picked up his briefcase. "Where are you originally from?"

"Michigan."

"Ah."

"Ah?"

"You have a way about you that's different.

Heat crept into her cheeks. "O-kay."

"I like it," he said.

His grin disarmed her. He really was handsome. How had she not realized that before? Sharp, cool and calm under pressure. His thick graying hair once had been very dark but the lighter strands were attractive. She liked the way the corners of his eyes crinkled when he smiled.

Lidia mentally stepped back and assessed the situation. He was a widower, like herself. They were colleagues, working toward a common goal. She'd seen him at church a few times. All pluses. Before she could talk herself out of it, she asked, "Want to grab a bite to eat?"

"Love to." He held the door open for her.

A confused mixture of pleasure and angst stretched through her system. "Great." Lidia walked out of the office and in the hall, very aware of Porter's hand at her elbow.

She couldn't believe it. She had just asked the D.A. out to dinner. She hadn't been on a date in at least five years and had no intention of starting a relationship beyond the confines of work.

So why was she so looking forward to the evening?

Two days after she'd first stepped onto the campus of Boston College, Anne found herself lugging Professor McClain's new notebook to his office on the second floor. She hefted the box a little higher so she could knock on the professor's door. She waited a moment before knocking again. When no reply came, she shifted the box to her hip and tried the door handle. Locked.

"Great," she muttered and bent to put the box on the floor. Once free of the encumbering box, she shook out her arms and stretched her back. She'd sent the good professor a note telling him she'd be delivering his computer at five o'clock, long after his last class of the day ended.

She checked her watch. Okay, so she was a few minutes early. Still.

She leaned against the smooth green-painted wall to wait. At least the halls were empty and peaceful. So far her job as a BC temp was going well. Boston College lay in the suburb of Newton, eight miles outside of Boston proper. Newton Center had lots of coffee houses and wonderful trinket shops. Plus a commuter train stop that could take her into Boston when she wanted. She really liked the area. Too bad she wouldn't be staying long.

And she hadn't come here without doing a little research. The current campus site on Chestnut Hill had been built in the early 1900s and featured examples of English Gothic architecture that Anne found fascinating. She'd spent countless hours wandering the walking paths that meandered through lush lawns and tall maples and evergreens to stare at the buildings.

There was something so…moving about the majestic structures with their cathedral-like shapes made of stone and mortar. Where she'd grown up houses were made of wood or tin. When she'd moved to the city, she'd found only a concrete jungle that both intimidated and awed her.

In this New England setting, she was content with her life. No matter how short her time here would be. She smothered the anger that sprouted. What was done was done, she had to learn to live with it.

A movement at the far end of the long, empty hallway made her push away from the wall. A man stood in the shadows at the top of the stairs. She couldn't make out his features. He didn't look tall enough or broad enough to be the professor. She squinted. "Professor McClain?"

"Yes?" a deep voice came from right beside her shoulder.

She jumped with a squeak and whirled around to face the professor. Tall, overbearing—and for some reason comforting. "What…?" Her gaze swung back to the shadows. No one was there. "Did you see that guy?"

"Who?" His gazed moved past her toward the stairwell.

Foreboding chased down her spine. She hadn't imagined the man in the shadows, she was sure of it. She tightened her hold on her purse, feeling the outline of her cell phone. Her lifeline. "No one, I guess."

Behind his glasses, Patrick's dark blue eyes regarded her with puzzlement. "Are you okay?"

She liked his eyes, liked how a darker shade of brown rimmed the irises, like layers of rich chocolate cake.

"Yes. Yes, I'm fine. Do you always sneak up on people?"

One side of his mouth twitched. "You sound like my sister-in-law, Kate. She's always accusing me of sneaking up on her. I can't help it if I'm light on my feet."

Anne gave his long, lean frame a once-over. "Dance classes?" she joked.

He shrugged and she thought his cheeks turned pink but in the waning light coming from the high window above the classroom doors she wasn't sure. "My mother thought her boys should be graceful."

"Cool mom," she commented as she bent to pick up the computer box. "Where I come from, boys would rather be hog-tied than sent to dance class."

"Here, allow me," Patrick said and bent as well, his hands covering hers on the box. Warm, big and strong.

"Where are you from?" he asked.

Slowly she withdrew her hands and straightened, aware of a funny little hitch in her breathing. Must still be the adrenaline from the man in the shadows making her forget herself.

"Al—L.A." She'd almost slipped up. That wouldn't be good.

"You're a long away from home."

He had no idea.

"Uh—" Patrick muttered as he stood with the box in his arms. "The door keys are in my pocket."

"No way am I going fishing," she stated and backed up a step. Three months ago, she would have expected that sort of line from practically every man she dealt with but not here, not now. Not the professor!

Patrick pinned her with a droll stare that made her think perhaps she'd overreacted. He balanced the box on one knee while he dug the keys from his coat pocket and held them out to her. "Here."

Taking the keys as embarrassed heat crept into her cheeks, she unlocked the door and pushed it open. Following Patrick inside, she looked around the office, not surprised to see a clean, clutter-free desk, faced by two perfectly aligned chairs and a filing cabinet with neatly written labels on each drawer. All button-down and tidy, just like the professor.

Patrick set the box on the corner of the desk. "I've backed up all my files. Twice."

She arched an eyebrow. "Really? On what?"

He went around the desk and opened a drawer to produce two floppy disks.

"Unfortunately your new computer doesn't take floppies."

His complexion paled. "It doesn't?"

He really was technologically challenged, which she found endearing. "CDs and thumb drives. Tomorrow I'll bring in a portable USB floppy drive."

He took his glasses off and began rubbing the lenses with a cloth. "That will solve the problem?"

"I'll have to save the files onto a thumb drive." She plucked a silver letter opener from the pen holder on the desk and went to work opening the box. "Until then, we can fire her up and see how she runs."

"You've given my computer a *female gender?*"

"We can call your computer a boy if you'd rather." She tugged on the white foam protector and slid the black notebook computer out of the box.

"The female pronoun is fine, like a ship. Just as potentially deadly and much too unpredictable."

"The same way guys view women," she stated and reached in the box for the cables.

"Excuse me?"

His affronted expression made her hold up her hand and amend her statement. She supposed it wasn't a fair statement, nor was it completely true. "Not all, just some."

He set his glasses back on his nose. "You're not old enough to have such a bleak outlook on the male gender."

She blinked. "Not old enough?"

"You're what, all of twenty?"

Her mouth twitched. "I'll take that as a compliment. Though I'm not sure you meant it as such. And I'm actually thirty." She ignored the fact that her current driver's license stated otherwise. What would it matter if he knew the truth?

He cocked his head. "Really? Indeed."

"Yes, indeed." She plugged the cable and cords into the right spots. "Here we go." She opened the lid of the laptop and began acquainting him with all the bells and whistles.

"So I can actually write on here with this little stick? And the computer types it in?"

She nodded, finding his amazement and wonder quite charming. "The stick is called a stylus and yes, the computer converts your writing to text. And," she said with a dramatic flare, "the lid folds all the way back so it looks more like a clipboard than a laptop, which makes writing on the pad that much easier."

"I think I'm going to like this."

Though there was a smile in his voice, his stoic expression didn't change. Odd. And odder still, she so wanted to see his smile.

She picked up her purse. "I'll leave you to play with your new toy. I'll come back tomorrow and download your files off that dinosaur." She gestured to the archaic computer taking up most of his desk.

He walked her to the door. "Thank you. I appreciate your up-to-date knowledge."

She hid a smile. He'd have a coronary if he knew that the basics of her knowledge came from a year of living with Rob, the computer geek, and the rest from the stack of manuals she'd been devouring over the last few weeks.

She was nothing if not a quick study. Would have been nice if the skill had helped with her acting career.

Moving to the Big Apple at seventeen to follow her dream of the Broadway stage hadn't worked out so well. She'd been just another pretty girl among a thousand other pretty girls, some with talent, others not so much. She'd been somewhere in the middle, but playing bit walk-on roles hadn't paid the bills.

Her dream of the theater had faded and reality had

set in. Clearly she'd had to adjust her plans and had found a way, besides acting, to survive.

But then again, the professor clearly didn't suspect she was anything other than what she presently appeared to be. Maybe she wasn't such a bad actress after all. That had to count for something.

"Uncle Raoul."

Raoul Domingo stared at his nephew Carlos and tightened his grip on the phone at his ear. He wanted to hit something or someone. But being incarcerated meant he had to hold on to his temper.

At least until he got out of the joint.

He still couldn't believe that female cop and her pretty boy partner had had the gall to bust in to his home in the middle of his dinner and cart him off in hand-cuffs.

As if he'd ever see the inside of a courtroom. No way! His men would make sure of that.

And then Raoul would settle the score with the two of them—especially the lady cop.

The Plexiglas window separating him from his nephew was dirty and scratched from years of standing between visitors and the inmates of New Jersey State Prison. Knowing their conversation was probably being recorded, he chose his words carefully so they couldn't incriminate him. He asked, "Have you taken care of that little detail?"

"Not yet."

Carlos squirmed under Raoul's furious stare. Raoul

wanted to reach through the glass and wrap his hands around his nephew's throat. "Get it done."

"We're working on it," Carlos assured him, his pockmarked face growing red.

"Work harder."

Carlos nodded. His gaze shifted around and he cupped a hand around the receiver. "We've got another issue."

Raoul's nostrils flared. "What?"

"My—uh, *friend* says there's another pigeon in the nest."

Acid churned in Raoul's gut. Another witnesss? How could that be? Trinidad had sworn the hotel was secure the night they'd visited Versailles, but apparently Raoul had been mistaken in trusting Trinidad. The man better come through now or he was dead meat.

"Tri—"

Raoul put his finger to his lips. "No names."

Carlos grimaced. "Yeah. Uh, we're out tracking."

Raoul wanted out of this stink hole so bad he could smell the tantalizing scent of freedom on his nephew. "Happy hunting."

TWO

Patrick paced the thick brown carpet of his office while the clicking of Anne's nails on the keyboard drilled into his head. She certainly knew her way around a computer and she seemed much more competent than his original assessment. Even so, it rankled knowing someone else had the power to destroy his work.

He didn't like uncertainty. He liked being in control. Had grown used to it since the day after his father died.

He'd become the man of the house, the guy his younger siblings turned to for advice or help and whom his mother relied upon to keep their world rotating even if the axis was now a bit skewed.

Patrick worried about his siblings, though Brody, who should be the one most messed up, had found a wonderful wife and now lived a great life. He'd somehow accepted the past and learned to live with the tragedy of their father's death.

Ryan had been too young to have been traumatized by their father's murder, but Patrick could see how much not having a father had pushed Ryan into his quest for material wealth. Patrick had a feeling Ryan thought having money would give him what he'd lacked as a child. Patrick wasn't so sure.

And then there was little Megan. Patrick adored his sister, but she most of all was messed up and not merely from the trauma of losing her dad, but she suffered from obsessive compulsive disorder, which was a bad combination with her fiercely independent spirit. As soon as she could, she'd left home to find her own place in the world.

Sometimes Patrick felt lost without his siblings underfoot. But he'd found a way to express his feelings in his work.

What if Anne lost something despite the CD and the little device she called a thumb drive? What if she inadvertently opened one of his files and read his writings? Would she laugh?

He could only pray that...

What a lame sentiment. As if God would listen.

No, Patrick couldn't rely on God to help, no matter how much his mother or his brother, Brody, tried to convince him otherwise.

So the best he could do was monitor computer-wizard Anne's progress.

A knock interrupted his thoughts. He opened the office door to a young Asian man, slim in build with dark, penetrating eyes that made Patrick think of onyx stones.

"Professor McClain?"

"Yes. Can I help you?"

The young man stuck out his hand. "My name is Cam. I'm transferring from MIT. I'll be taking your class, Macro Economics of the Irish, this summer." For a man with a slight frame, he had a strong grip.

"Wonderful." Why was he here now? Students didn't normally come knocking. Obviously this was an overeager overachiever. Not many of them around anymore. Too many students seemed jaded and uninterested in more than how to make a quick buck. "Do you have the list of required textbooks?"

"Yep. I'm all set. Just putting a face to the name on the syllabus," Cam stated with a pleasant smile. "I—"

"Oh, bummer!" Anne's voice interrupted.

Patrick glanced at Anne. She was shaking her head, her gaze fixated on the new computer screen. "Problem?" he asked.

She nodded but didn't look toward the door.

Wanting to end the interruption, he turned back to Cam and asked, "Is there anything else I can help you with tonight?"

Cam shook his head, his gaze riveted on Anne. "No, thank you."

"Okay, then." Patrick stepped into the man's line of vision.

Those obsidian eyes shifted to meet his gaze. "I'll see you in class, Professor."

As Patrick shut the door behind his new student, a chill skated across his flesh. There was something odd about Cam, something in the way the black of his eyes seemed depthless. Overeager, overachiever and off balance? He'd have to watch the guy. Patrick didn't want a Virginia Tech tragedy happening at Boston College.

Shaking off the strange notion as nothing more than his worry over his work, he turned his attention to Anne. Her bright red, spiked hair didn't look nearly as stiff tonight, as if she'd run her fingers through the points, loosening their rigidness.

Her high forehead creased with concentration and her lips moved without audible sound. The jacket of her ill-fitting brown suit hung off her shoulders, making her look slightly stooped.

"Why the bummer?" he asked as he came to stand at her side.

She sighed as she sat back. Her right hand reached up to massage her neck. "I zipped your files together and changed them to RTF. I just ran a program to import them to the new system and the computer didn't like it."

"That doesn't sound good." Patrick tried to keep a quiver of panic from seeping into his tone. If he lost his work now, he'd have a hard time retrieving it.

"It's not," she replied.

Heart beating in his throat, he asked, "Have I lost anything?"

"No."

Breathing more normally now, he relaxed slightly. "What exactly is wrong and how do we fix it?"

She turned her purple gaze on him. "Your old

computer software program is not talking nicely to the new software program. During the transfer, the formatting was lost. I can go in manually to each file and correct the formatting. It will just take some time."

"How much time?"

"A day, two at the most." She clicked open a file. "See."

The text on the screen was from one of his fall lectures, that much he could tell, but the words were all jumbled with paragraph breaks and tab spaces and what looked like hieroglyphics. He pointed to the screen. "What are all those?"

"Computer language. The new system has converted some of the letters and symbols. It's easy enough to read through and correct by deleting and replacing each symbol. But I can't do a global search and replace."

"This is bad," Patrick stated and plucked his glasses off his face to rub with a cloth he withdrew from his pocket.

Anne stood and placed a hand on his arm. "It's not dire, just time consuming."

The spot where her hand rested on his arm fired his senses beneath his sports coat. He cleared his throat. "You'll have to come back tomorrow then?"

"Yes. And I think I should start first thing in the morning, if you don't mind?"

Staring at the smooth, elegant fingers on his arm, he said, "The morning will be fine. I have a department retreat off campus until late afternoon."

She removed her hand and began shutting down the

computers. Patrick replaced his glasses and watched her movements. Efficient, graceful. Competent. Not at all like he'd first thought.

When the office was locked up for the night, Patrick handed his office key to Anne. "Can I walk you to your car?"

She put the key in her purse. "Actually I'm headed to the cafeteria. But thank you, Professor."

"I'm not really a professor." Now why had he blurted that out?

Her eyebrows rose. "You're not?"

"I'm only an associate professor." Heat rode up his neck.

She gave a small laugh. "But you're still a professor."

"True, just not a full professor."

"Okay. And you're telling me this…why?"

"You can call me Patrick."

"Oh. Well, then. Good night, Patrick," she said, giving him an odd look before hurrying away.

Patrick could just imagine his father shaking his head and saying, *Smooth, boy-o.*

A sadness that always burned just below the surface bubbled, reminding Patrick of all he'd lost. Reminding him of all he could lose if he ever let himself care too deeply ever again.

Anne paid the cafeteria cashier for her meal of egg salad sandwich, side garden salad and a bottle of water. One of the perks of temping at the college was the food discount in the cafeteria, though under the harsh fluorescent lights the egg salad had a greenish tinge that wasn't terribly appealing. But she'd had one a few days earlier and had enjoyed it, so she wasn't going to let a little green rob her of her dinner.

Halfway through her meal, she had the strange sense of being watched. Her gaze swung over the few other late evening diners and landed on the student who'd come to Professor McClain's door. Cam, he'd said his name was, stood near the vending machine, his lean, wiry frame still and his black eyes boring holes right through her.

She frowned, hoping to convey her displeasure at being stared at.

He turned abruptly and put his money in the machine. Once he had a can of soda in hand, he moved out the door and into the dusky night.

A shiver of recognition slithered along Anne's arms, prickling her skin. She was sure he'd been the man standing in the shadows yesterday.

Was his claim of putting the professor's face to his name true? Was Cam really a transfer student or someone more sinister? Had she been found? Would she have to run again? Where would she go? How far would she have to flee to be safe?

"Stop being paranoid," she muttered to herself.

But just in case, she'd like to be safe inside the four walls of her apartment.

Gathering her belongings, she quickly left the cafeteria. The balmy June air bathed her, sending the last of the air-conditioned chill of the cafeteria away with a shiver.

Glancing around to be sure no one followed, she hurried to her four-door sedan parked beneath one of the tall parking lot lamps.

As she drove, once again taking a different route to her street, she pulled out her cell phone and pushed the speed-dial number for the one person who wouldn't think she was totally off her rocker for being paranoid.

"It's me," Anne said to the woman who'd picked up the line.

"What's the matter?" The sharp edge of concern echoed in Lieutenant Taylor's voice.

"Nothing, I think. I don't know. I'm just getting antsy."

"You wouldn't call just because you were antsy."

"You said to call if anything seemed out of sync. This student...I don't know. He gives me the creeps. There's something vaguely familiar about him."

"Do you have a name?"

"Cam. That's all I got. He said he's a transfer student from MIT. He's taking one of Professor McClain's classes this summer."

"I'll check into it." There was a moment of silence. "How's it going with the professor? Is he as stodgy as his profile says?"

Anne hesitated. Stodgy? After spending so many hours with him, that wasn't a word she'd use to describe him. Cute for a geek. Adorably nerdy. Definitely charming in an odd way. Maybe too charming. Too easy to get caught up in. *You can call me Patrick.* "He's an academic. Just the titles of his published articles make me yawn."

An indelicate snort met her statement. "Don't get attached. You'll be leaving there soon."

Anne sighed. "I know. Thanks for the reminder." As if she could forget. "How soon?"

"Hard to say. The D.A. has you scheduled to testify right before closing arguments so you won't have to come back to New Jersey until them."

"How's the trial going so far?"

"Slow. I'll be in touch. And, hey…"

"Yes?"

"Everything's going to be all right. You'll get through this, you know You're strong."

The reassurance soothed some of Anne's tension. If only she felt strong. "Thanks."

"Call if anything else strange happens. You can always reach me at this number."

"Will do."

Anne clicked off and tried for some deep, calming breaths as she pulled her car into her parking space right in front of her building door.

Inside the safety of her studio apartment, Anne was greeted by a large white Persian cat with only one eye and a pink collar sporting a dangling, sparkly tiara charm.

Relaxing her voice, Anne said, "Hello, sugar." She

picked the cat up and snuggled her close. For a moment Princess allowed the contact before squirming to get away. Anne set the cat back on the floor with a sigh. Sometimes she wasn't sure if the cat loved her or not.

A few days after moving to Boston she'd gone to the humane society looking for a guard dog and ended up with a cat. The minute she'd seen the feline, she fell in love with the ball of fluff named Princess and had brought her home.

Princess marched straight to her bowl, tail stuck in the air, and meowed.

"Ah, we're hungry." Anne opened a can of food and left Princess to her dinner.

Making her way over to the Murphy bed, Anne kicked off her shoes and stretched her toes. She hated heels, but the role she was playing required sensible pumps and the itchy dress suit. Thankfully bare legs were an acceptable style. The thought of nylons made her shudder.

She changed into soft cotton pajamas and crawled under the down comforter. Her mind wouldn't quiet down however. Her thoughts kept churning through the morass of danger that lurked. Was Cam a student or a henchman for Raoul Domingo? Would one of them slit her throat as she slept? As she came out of the school building? Went to the grocery store? Would she ever feel safe?

And what of the professor? And how much she enjoyed being around him?

Thinking about Patrick was more productive than angsting about the threat she couldn't control.

There was something very steady and reassuring about him that drew her in and made her wish he could see her as she really was.

But he might not be so nice to her then.

The social-status-conscious "associate" professor wouldn't want to socialize with a woman who had barely passed high school and had grown up in a trailer in the backwoods.

She punched the pillow with a groan. The sooner she got his computer up and running, the sooner she could move on to another project and another professor before her time was up in Boston.

She couldn't afford to get too chummy with anyone. Or "attached."

She was pretty sure she could keep from revealing her past, but she wasn't sure that she could keep her lonely heart from wanting what she couldn't have.

A friend. Love. A life without fear.

As one day turned in to two days of deleting, replacing and reformatting, Anne's eyes stung with grit and fatigue stiffened the muscles in her neck and shoulders. She'd figured out how to convert the old computer software into a language the new software could easily and readily read, but just to be on the safe side she'd been reading through each file and would occasionally find a trouble spot that she had to manually correct.

Though the subject matter of economics wasn't something she found interesting, she'd certainly learned a lot. There was one file that looked huge and she'd been saving it for last.

She glanced at the computer clock. She should be able to finish with the files and get the docking station set up before Patrick returned to his office.

She clicked to open the file, "Turned Up Side Down" expecting to see more charts, theories and statistics, but instead she found herself staring at a work of fiction.

A novel. Written by Patrick McClain.

Both curiosity and the desire to make sure the file hadn't lost all of its formatting urged her to read.

Fascination kept her glued to the words.

Soon she was hooked into the story of a young boy who loses his father and must step into the role of man of the house.

She laughed at the antics of the boy and his siblings and fought tears of empathy for the characters. She reached the last page with a satisfied sigh, yet knew she'd seen some formatting issues but she'd been so engrossed in the story that she hadn't wanted to stop reading to fix.

She'd have to read through it again. She rubbed at her eyes. It would be easier if she could read the words from a hard copy. She began printing off the book, while her mind raced with thoughts of the story and Patrick.

She realized she knew very little of his private life.

Was this book autobiographical or purely fiction? If autobiographical, she was in deep trouble.

Weren't damaged hearts notorious for falling for their like?

After his meeting with the department chair, Patrick headed to his office, expecting to find Anne waiting for him with his computer ready to go and trusting his files to be intact.

Instead he found his office door wide-open and Anne sitting in his chair, her fingers clicking on the keyboard. Off to the side his printer hummed as it rhythmically spat pages into the tray.

Patrick couldn't help the little glow of approval in his gut for how hard the woman worked. A very admirable trait. She definitely had surpassed his expectations, her fashion choices notwithstanding.

Tonight, though, she wore another ill-fitting, conservative dress suit, and her spiked hair seemed especially...barbed. Her normally creamy complexion held a hint of makeup and beneath her dark lashes, circles of fatigue marred her delicate skin.

She glanced up. Her wary smile made him feel as if he'd walked in on something he shouldn't have.

"Hello." He stepped through the doorway and hovered near the desk.

"Uh—hi. I'm sorry, I had hoped to be done by now. This last file has been sticky."

"No problem." He glanced at the printer. "What's this?"

"Your book."

Distress grabbed his throat as he reached for the top page. He barely glanced at the words. His agitation increased until shock and rage choked him.

She was printing his book.

"How could you?"

THREE

The sharpness of his voice made Anne push the chair back, creating more distance between them. He suddenly looked too broad and too muscular for the herringbone sport jacket and tan pants he wore. "Excuse me?"

He crumbled the paper in his hands. "You read my personal file."

Very carefully, she stated, "I've been checking all the files for formatting errors and I simply needed to print this one out and read it again because it's so big. I thought you were aware of what I needed to do."

"Well…I didn't…you shouldn't have," he sputtered.

Gone was the mild-mannered, geeky professor, replaced with a hard-jawed stranger and the storm clouds gathering in his dark eyes warned he was about to blow a gasket.

Yet every line in his face and every nuance of his body spoke of self-control.

Anne stood, her legs steady and her mind calm. Facing an irate academic was nothing compared to the business end of a gun. "Your book is good. Really good."

"This was private." He grabbed the papers from the printer tray and dumped them into the wastebasket.

"No," Anne cried, latching on to the can. "Look, I'm sorry. But don't do this. You have talent."

He tugged on the can until she let go. "Finish what you need to and get out."

Reeling as if he'd slapped her, she could only stare at him as he turned on his loafer-clad heel and left the office, trash can in hand.

"Fine," she muttered, her own anger sparking brightly. She'd only been trying to help. She didn't need him. They were just ships passing in the nightmare of her life.

Quickly she finished setting up the docking station for the laptop. Monday she'd have to ask Sharon to help Professor McClain set up his e-mail with his passwords and such, because obviously they weren't going to be able to work together anymore.

When she was done, she locked up behind her and hurried out of the darkened building. She pushed open the main entrance doors that faced the lot where she'd parked, to find a man sat on the top stair. She hesitated as fear snaked around her, squeezing her lungs, until she realized who sat there.

"Professor?" she managed to squeak.

He stood. "Call me Patrick, please." His features

appeared more angular in the glow of the overhead path lights. "I'm sorry. My behavior was inexcusable."

Touched by the humble sincerity in his voice, she admitted, "You were in the right."

"I shouldn't have growled at you."

"I shouldn't have read and printed off your book without asking you, since it clearly wasn't part of your teaching material."

"Regardless, that gave me no right to treat you so poorly."

She arched an eyebrow. What just went down was his idea of treating her poorly? Okay, was the man a saint or just so well-bred that showing anger was considered bad manners?

She'd take his idea of poor treatment any day over the way her father had treated her mother.

Anne shuddered at the memories flipping through her mind. Her father had been a mean, pious drunk and her mother a passive enabler who'd been too tired from caring for five kids to do more than crawl into her own bottle of gin.

Anne's subsequent experiences with men weren't much better. Her first boyfriend, Johnny, had had a temper that earned him the nickname bruiser on the football field. He'd treated her no less gently.

She'd hoped when she escaped the backwoods into the Big Apple she'd find decent guys who would treat her with respect. There'd been Drew, Simon and Greg. Not one had met her high expectations.

Not willing to blithely walk away from this rare

gem in her life, she said, "How about we let it go and you walk me to my car." She dared to loop her arm through his.

There was a moment of stiff hesitation before he covered her hand on his arm. "I would be happy to."

Trying not to notice the ribbons of comforting heat unfurling through her veins, Anne's gaze searched the parking lot for her car.

She mentally paused. Something wasn't right. Three of the parking lot's overhead lamps were out. Her car wasn't under any of the ten remaining lit lamps.

Coincidence? She wanted to think so, but a deep, gut-wrenching awareness lifted the hairs at her nape.

You're being paranoid, she scolded herself. Still, her footsteps faltered.

"Anne?"

She halted. "Are you parked over here?"

"I'm in the faculty lot behind the building."

He'd think she was nuts if she told him she was afraid to walk to her car because the light she'd parked under was out, and knowing how much he valued logic, she said, "It would make more sense if we go to your car first and then you drive me over here. That way you don't have to double back. And the school exit is right there."

He dipped his head in thoughtful acknowledgment. "That does make sense."

Anne breathed a sigh of relief as they turned around, but she couldn't stop the chill chasing its way across her flesh as she flung a glance over her shoulder toward the darkened parking space where her car waited.

From the back of the sedan, a man watched with growing anger as Anne and the professor stopped for a moment before walking in the opposite direction and disappeared around the corner of the building. He swore graphically as he unfolded himself from the back seat and got out of the car.

He wouldn't be grabbing anyone tonight.

Since the car had held little information, he knew tonight's work was a bust.

But that didn't mean he couldn't send a message that would give the little rat something to think about.

"I hadn't pictured you as the Mini Cooper type," Anne commented as Patrick shifted into Reverse and backed the small coupe out of his parking spot. "I'd have thought you more of a Volvo guy."

He grunted in acknowledgment. "I bought it for my mother when she expressed interest in driving, but then she changed her mind," he replied, his tone echoed with resignation as he drove toward the front parking lot.

"And you ended up with the car." She stretched her legs, surprised by the amount of room in the vehicle. "Your mother doesn't drive at all?"

"Not at all. Any place she wants to go that she can't walk to or ride the T to, she has someone take her."

"That someone being you?"

He shook his head. "No. She has a whole network of people to chauffeur her around."

Anne couldn't fathom that type of dependence on others.

The headlights of Patrick's Mini Cooper splashed across Anne's car. She sucked in a shocked breath.

"What in the world...?"

Patrick's exclamation of surprise chased the fear sliding down her spine.

The front and side windows had been reduced to jagged holes with sharp glass teeth, a flat tire made the car sit low to the ground and list slightly to the left. The taillights and headlights littered the ground with pieces of colored plastic and glass.

"Oh, thank you, Jesus," she breathed out, grateful she'd heeded the internal alert that had warned her not to walk to the car in the dark.

"You're thanking God for someone vandalizing your car?"

She couldn't make out Patrick's features but she heard the incredulous tone of his voice. How did she explain something she didn't fully understand?

"Do you believe in God?" she countered.

There was a moment of tense silence before he near growled, "Yes."

Abruptly he got out of his car and walked toward her smashed up car, leaving Anne with the distinct impression that he'd had to think about his answer.

Did he really believe? In his heart or just his head? Why did it matter to her?

Don't get attached. She had to remember that.

She got out and walked over to the destruction where Patrick was now examining the tires.

"Slashed."

A feeling of violation choked Anne.

Patrick unclipped a cell phone from the belt at his waist and reported the vandalism. "The police are on their way."

"Thank you for calling them and for being here," she managed to say around the lump in her throat.

"Let's wait in my car." Patrick touched her elbow, the pressure reassuring as he led her back to the coupe.

Once they were settled in, he said, "Well, this was bound to happen."

"Excuse me?" Did he know? How could he? Un-less...

"What college do you know of that doesn't have to deal with some negative elements? I just hope it doesn't escalate into something worse."

Anne sighed and let her forehead rest against the side window and stared out at the night sky. "Let's hope not."

"Not that I'm discounting the vandalism to your car, but I'm glad no one was hurt."

So was she.

Two blue and white Newton police cruisers pulled up and two sets of officers evacuated the cars.

Patrick went to meet them.

Anne took the opportunity to make a call.

"Anne?" Lieutenant Taylor's voice brought her a measure of comfort.

"My car was broken into. Professor McClain called the police and they've arrived."

"Was there anything in the car that had your personal information on it?"

"No, I don't think so." She tried to mentally picture the contents of the car. The candy bar wrapper from the other day. Her travel coffee mug in the holder. Nothing else.

"Good. That's good. Don't worry, Anne. There's no way anyone could find you. I want you to call me when you get home."

"Okay." She hung up, praying that her trust was well placed.

She got out of the car, her gaze searching the dark shadows of the college.

An older officer approached her with a notebook in hand. The name on his badge was O'Sullivan. "Miss, we need you to check to see what's missing."

She shook her head. "There wasn't anything in the car."

"Do you know of anyone who has a grudge against you?"

She swallowed. Yes, but she was sworn not to say anything. "I've only recently moved to the area. I know hardly anyone."

"Have you had any troubles here?"

"No, everyone I've met has been very nice." She thought about the student named Cam. She debated mentioning him, but she'd trust that he was already being investigated.

"Hey, O'Sullivan, we've got two more cars here with the same type of damage."

O'Sullivan flipped closed his notebook. "Well, that puts a different spin on the situation. You weren't a target, only a random victim."

Anne's shoulders sagged with relief. Random she could deal with.

Patrick, who had been talking to one of the other officers, stepped closer. "Does she need to file a report tonight or can she come to the station tomorrow?"

"Tomorrow's fine. I'd make sure you call your insurance company right away and have them tow your car to a repair shop." The officer turned back to Patrick. "How's your brother, Brody doing?"

"Good. Soon to be a dad."

"You tell him congratulations. Does Gabe know?"

Patrick shrugged. "Not sure."

Interesting that the police knew Patrick's family. She wondered what the connection was.

Anne left the two men talking to walk to the passenger side of her car, glass crunching under her heels. She opened the glove box. Empty. Her heart stalled then pounded in painful beats as she hurried back to the officer.

"The insurance card and the registration are both gone." She couldn't keep trepidation from creeping into her voice. The pertinent information on both items listed a post office box address in the downtown branch of the Boston Post Office. She clearly wouldn't be going to the post office anytime soon.

O'Sullivan's brow creased and his light eyes showed concern. "Give me your address and I'll have Johnny and Mic secure the premises before you arrive."

She swallowed back a flutter of panic. She couldn't very well tell them that she couldn't be traced by the information, which would only lead to questions she couldn't answer.

Better to be safe and let the officers check her apartment. She gave O'Sullivan her address.

"We'll follow the officers," Patrick stated and put his hand on the small of Anne's back.

She took comfort from his strength and allowed him to escort her to his car. Once they were driving out of the parking lot, she dropped her head back on the headrest. The need to confide in Patrick rose sharply, but she forced it down.

She couldn't tell him who she was or why she was here; doing so could jeopardize not only her life but his.

Patrick pulled up behind the police cruiser and watched the two officers enter Anne's building. Very few lights glowed from the many window of the brick structure. The black metal fire escapes made darker slashes in the shadows.

Near the front door two huge arborvitaes grew at least ten feet in the air, blocking the two side lights and providing good cover for someone waiting in the dark to ambush a person going in or out.

Patrick wasn't usually prone to such suspicious thinking. One of his younger brothers, Brody, a sheriff on Nantucket, was the one who'd followed in their father's footsteps by going into law enforcement. But Patrick figured the events of the night must have triggered some latent cop genes.

In the dim light of the moon coming through the windows of the car, Patrick could make out the tightness around Anne's mouth and the worry marring her brow. Protectiveness surged, surprising him with its intensity.

Being protective and responsible for others was part of who he was, but this was...different.

He refused to analyze the possible explanations now and instead covered her hand with his.

She met his gaze and gave him a wan smile. "I'm sorry you have to deal with all of this."

"It's not your fault, and I will be here as long as you need me." And he meant it, which surprised him even more. He liked life to be predictable and uneventful, which didn't seem to happen around Anne.

The two officers came out of the building and approached the car. Patrick gave Anne's hand a reassuring squeeze before they got out to hear what the officers had discovered.

"The place is clear. We checked the halls of each floor and the back of the building. There's no way for anyone to get inside without the access codes," the taller of the two, Officer Nelson, said.

"Will you patrol the area anyway?" Patrick asked,

aware that Anne had rounded the car and stood slightly off to the side.

The shorter officer, Buggetti, nodded. "Sure. We'll stay in the area tonight and put a request in for regular drive-bys."

"Thank you gentlemen." Patrick shook the officers' hands.

"Thank you, officers," Anne echoed as they passed by her on the way to their vehicle.

When the patrol car disappeared from view, Anne turned to Patrick. "Thanks again for everything."

"Uh, sure," Patrick responded. Her words were a dismissal but he wasn't ready yet to leave her; logic dictated that he made sure she got into her apartment safely. "I'll walk you in."

"You don't have to. The officers said all was fine."

"I know I don't have to. I want to."

She blinked, surprise shining in her violet eyes. "Okay. Well, that's fine."

He followed her inside the brick five-story walk-up. All was quiet as they climbed the linoleum covered stairs to the third floor. At the fourth door to the right, Anne stopped and unlocked the door before turning to face him.

"Again, thank you. I'll be by Monday to show you how to use the docking station and help you set up your password accounts," she said.

"How will you get there?"

"Uh— Transit. Or a cab."

She looked scared, tired and in need of a shoulder

to lean on. Not to mention a ride. Amazingly he wanted to be that shoulder even though doing so would only complicate his life.

Time for you to get a life, Patrick.

Maybe it was time for that. But did he really want to start with Anne and the burden of responsibility he already felt toward her?

Spending time with her didn't mean he was looking for a romance. They could be friends. They could both use a friend. And friendship wasn't a burden.

He placed a hand on the door frame next to her head. "I'll come pick you up. But in the meantime, is there anywhere you need to go this weekend?"

"No, I just plan to veg out. Well, actually, on Sunday morning I plan to go to church."

Patrick straightened, his chest knotting. "Is it close by?"

She shook her head. Her pretty eyes studied his face. "Would you be willing to take me?"

He took in as much air as his cramped chest would allow. Take her to church? To a house of God?

But he'd offered to take her anywhere she needed to go. Was he now going to put conditions on that offer? His honor wouldn't allow it.

"Yes. I'll take you to church."

Standing in the shadows outside of the apartment building, the man stood waiting to see which lights went on so he'd know which apartment the woman lived in.

Following the cops and the other pair in their little car had been a stroke of luck. He couldn't have planned it better.

Ah, there was the light. Third floor, fourth set of windows. The front door of the building opened and the professor came out. The man pulled back into the shadows until the Mini Cooper was out of sight.

With a cheeky grin, he took out his enhanced state-of-the-art PDA computer system and uplinked to a sophisticated server that, in his hands, would very quickly give him the information he needed.

He might as well have a little fun with his prey before he killed her.

FOUR

Sunday morning arrived with a beautiful forecast of a sunny day topped with a cooling June breeze.

"What do you think, sugar?" Anne asked Princess, who sat on the edge of the Murphy bed, her one eye regarding Anne and the blue polka-dot skirt she held up for inspection. Anne shrugged and turned back to the closet. "Maybe too flowing."

She sighed and fingered the drab business suits she'd been wearing every day to the college. She really didn't like the itchy suits, but she had a role to play. And today was no different since Patrick would be coming soon to pick her up to take her to church. She hoped he'd like the place and the service. She'd been a tad apprehensive when her super, Mr. Bonaro, had recommended it. But she'd instantly felt welcome and safe among the congregation.

A ripple of anxiety and excitement went through her and she jumped on the bed, grabbing Princess along the way. The cat squirmed and then settled into the crook of Anne's neck.

"I really shouldn't be doing this," Anne told the cat. "But I couldn't resist. There's something about Patrick that I like."

Princess meowed and scrambled out of Anne's arms, jumped off the bed and skidded to a halt at the front door where she pawed at the crack underneath. Anne hurried to the door, hoping Patrick hadn't shown up early. She couldn't see anyone through the peephole.

Swallowing a bout of trepidation, Anne cracked open the door. Her stomach rolled. She put her hand over her mouth as she gagged. A rodent laid in the middle of the hall, its neck broken.

"Gross!" She slammed the door shut.

After getting control of her stomach, she called Mr. Bonaro and demanded he come right away.

With a glance at the clock, Anne grabbed a brown dress suit and quickly dressed. She prayed that the super would get rid of the rat before Patrick showed up. Having a dead rat on her doorstep wouldn't make a good impression.

Just as she slipped on her heels, there was a knock on the door. She peered out the peephole. The super.

She cracked opened the door. Vigilo Bonaro barely reached Anne's shoulder. His stooped sixty-plus years frame looked frail but Anne had seen the man heft the full garbage cans in the back alley like they weighed nothing. His wrinkled face was screwed up in disgust. In his hand he held a dark plastic bag that hung heavy with the body of the dead rat. "I got it." He held up the bag.

"Did the...animal have teeth marks?" she asked, avoiding looking at the bag.

He shrugged. "I no inspect it." He nodded his head toward Princess, who'd come to sit at her feet. "Your cat, she bring you gift, no?"

"No. Princess is an indoor cat." She shuddered. "But I'll bet the guy in 3B's terrier could have done this. That dog is always running loose."

"I ask him next time I see him," Mr. Bonaro assured her.

"You don't think there could be more of them around, do you?" Her gaze searched the corridor.

Mr. Bonaro shook his head. "No." He shrugged. "But just in case, I call exterminator."

"Great. I appreciate you taking care of it."

He nodded and ambled away with the plastic bag swinging at his side.

Anne shuddered with revulsion. She quickly made sure Princess had food and water and then grabbed her purse and headed downstairs to wait on the street.

Just as she stepped outside, Patrick's Mini Cooper pulled up. He got out and came around the car to open the door for her. She drank in the sight of his tall, lean build clothed in pressed slacks and an oxford button-down shirt and tie. His dark slightly damp hair curled adorably at the ends and his strong, clean-shaven jaw made her want to reach out and draw her finger along that straight line.

"Good morning," Patrick greeted her, pulling her out of her momentary stupor.

He held open the passenger door. As she passed him she caught a whiff of his aftershave. A pleasing, clean spicy scent.

"Hi. Sorry. I'm still waking up," she said and slipped inside the car.

When he was settled in the driver's seat, he said, "Where to?"

She gave him directions. She thought about telling him of the rat incident but then decided not to taint his morning as well. She wanted him to be open to God's word, not thinking about her living conditions. She was having enough trouble banishing the image from her own mind.

She prayed that the rodent wasn't a bad omen of things to come.

Patrick walked slowly with Anne toward the Newton Community Church entrance. The old stone building stood on a parcel of land on the edge of town. Lush lawns and a beautiful garden made the whole scene picturesque, too perfect to be genuine. People gathered along the walkways, greeting each other with smiles and well-wishes. Had he stepped into the land of the Stepfords?

Several people said hello to Anne as they passed and she introduced him. Patrick nodded his greeting as the knot on the tie at his neck seemed to pull tighter with each passing moment.

He just wanted this over with so they could leave as soon as possible. He didn't want to have to engage in conversation with these seemingly happy people. He didn't want to be here. Church brought back too many memories.

Memories of times with his father as the family headed off to their church.

Memories of how his father would loop his arm over Patrick's shoulder and walk beside him across the park to the building where they worshipped.

Memories of the day he'd been told of his father's death. He'd run off, across the park to the one place he'd always felt peace. The church.

He didn't feel peace in or out of church anymore. He probably never would and pretending he did only made the ache in his soul that much sharper.

But he'd said he'd take Anne anywhere she wanted to go, so he here was.

Anne led him to a row of padded chairs.

"Do we have to sit up front?" He scanned the outer aisles, wishing he could slip out the side door.

Her big violet eyes widened slightly. "No, I guess not. I just always do. We can move back if you'd rather."

He sighed and sat. "This is fine."

Still standing, she stared at him with concern. "Are you sure? I don't mind moving back."

He took her hand and tugged her into the seat next to him. Her soft, supple skin against his palm warmed him. He loosened his grip, expecting her to withdraw but instead she hung on, confusing his senses and ringing an alarm in his brain that he chose to ignore because her touch both soothed and distracted him.

For this moment he would allow the closeness and emotional connection arcing between them. It blotted out the heartache of loss that was lurking always below his surface and was trying to rise even now. He squeezed her hand and she smiled, distracting him more.

The inside of the chapel was as beautiful as the outside, with high arches and multicolored stained-glass windows. A stage at the front of the sanctuary was equipped with musical instruments. Four standing microphones and a portal pulpit off to the side. Much different than what he was used to. There were no candelabras, no pipe organ or altar. Maybe this was a concert and not a church service.

Wouldn't that be great. He could handle that.

Anne slipped her hand away as the young woman sitting behind them passed Anne a program. He missed the contact of Anne's hand and declined the program offered to him. Within a few moments all the seats filled and a group of people took their places at the equipment on stage. Patrick pulled at his tie.

The band began to play and the singers joined in. Over the heads of the singers the words of the songs were projected onto the wall.

Hymns.

Patrick recognized the words and the tunes but the songs had been rearranged to an upbeat, contemporary tempo.

Fascinating.

Beside him, Anne's voice rang clear. He listened,

mesmerized by the quality of her tone. There was something different about the way she sang as opposed to the way she talked. He tried to decipher what it was, but soon found himself listening to the words and watching serenity steal over Anne's expression.

The songs of God's love and grace resonated with some chord inside Patrick. Emotions and feelings he'd long ago rejected rose, refusing to be batted down. He wanted to run from the room, he wanted to break down, he wanted to kneel before God and ask, "Why? Why did you let my father die?"

Controlling his emotions and his feelings was something Patrick had mastered as a young boy, but it took every ounce of self-possession to get them under control now.

He would not feel. He would not allow God back into his heart. He hurt too much. His family had suffered too much.

When the music ended and the pulpit had been moved to the front of the stage by a man roughly Patrick's age, whom he accurately guessed was the pastor, Patrick turned to stare out the window at the green grass and blue sky. He didn't want to be there, didn't want to hear what the man had to say about God. Patrick would tune the pastor out, like he did Pastor James whenever Patrick gave in and allowed his mother to drag him with her to church.

Movement in his peripheral vision drew his attention to Anne. She had a notepad and pen in hand and was writing. She wrote the reference of Job 5:7.

Patrick remembered the story of Job. God allowed Satan to test Job's faith by taking everything away from him.

Anne continued to write, and against his better judgment, Patrick began to listen to the message. The pastor's voice had a fluid rhythm and his inflections smoothed Patrick's unease.

"Each of us will face real pain, disappointment and loss."

A deep, biting sensation in Patrick's midsection caught him by surprise. He refrained from clutching at his gut.

"The world says you are either loved by God and saved or you are hated by God and made to suffer adversity. Job's friends told him that all adversity comes from sin. But God answered that belief with His own words and rebuked Job's friends. We must know and accept that adversity is part of human life, which faith overcomes."

Patrick dropped his gaze to his shoes; his breathing turned shallow. Faith. He'd had faith once. Had deeply trusted God. But then God had betrayed that trust. How could this pastor say that faith overcame adversity?

"When we lose someone we love, our lives are changed. Change is a part of life. But healing begins when we acknowledge that loss and risk loving again."

Patrick's chest constricted until taking a breath became impossible. He had to escape.

Patrick lurched to his feet and stumbled to the side

door where he escaped into the fresh air. Sucking in big, gulping breaths, he tried to reason out the logic of his reaction, but his mind refused to focus on anything other than the words reverberating inside his head.

Faith overcomes adversity.

Risk loving again.

Accept adversity.

He rubbed at him temples. He couldn't accept what happened to his father because doing so would force him to face the loss. Facing that loss would rip him apart.

He had to remain strong for his mother and siblings. He'd become the man of the house after his father died. Everyone had expected him to be brave and not show his pain. All of his father's fellow officers had encouraged and approved of Patrick's strength. Patrick didn't know how to be anything else.

Our lives are changed.

No kidding.

"Patrick, what's wrong?"

Anne's concerned voice forced him to regain control of himself. Squaring his shoulders, he turned to face her. The tender regard in her gaze nearly made his knees buckle. He wanted to reach out to her for comfort, but he didn't know how. He'd always been the one to offer comfort and support.

"I'm fine. You should go back in. I'll wait at the car."

She touched his arm, her hand searing him to his

soul. "You're not fine. Did you have an asthma attack? I could hear how hard you were breathing."

If only asthma were the problem. But he nodded. "I couldn't breathe for a moment. I'm really fine now."

She squeezed his arm before dropping her hand. "We can leave now."

"You should stay and finish the service."

"The service is almost over anyway, and I'd rather be with you."

The corner of his lip curled up and gladness touched his heart. "I like the sound of that."

"Do you have plans for the rest of the day?"

"No." Mom had gone to see Brody and his wife Kate for the weekend. He had no one else to spend time with.

"Would you be up for a trip into Boston, maybe take the Duck Tour?"

The water and land tour via a World War II amphibious landing vehicle was a popular Boston tourist attraction. "I haven't done that since I was young." They'd gone as a family when he was six. He cherished the memory.

"I've been wanting to do it ever since I moved here, but just haven't taken the time. So are you game?"

He glanced at her. Spending the day with Anne sure beat going home to an empty apartment or back to his office to wallow in the emotions the church service had stirred up. "I'd love to."

Her pleased smile knocked his senses for a loop. *Risk loving again.*

But love came with risk. And loss. He didn't want

to ever feel that pain again. It was only logical that he kept an emotional barrier between them.

Excitement bubbled inside Anne's chest as she and Patrick boarded the bright yellow amphibious landing vehicle. She couldn't believe she was spending the day with Patrick.

The outside of the beast was metal and, according to the brochure, watertight. A canvas awning attached to two poles on either end offered shade to the occupants. Inside, rows of padded bench seats waited.

She and Patrick sat toward the front. He gave her the window seat, which she appreciated since the view was better. His shoulder brushed against hers as they settled in. She didn't scoot farther away, instead shifted ever so slightly to increase the contact. He felt so good next to her, a shield she could finally hide behind.

The tour guide, or rather conductor as he preferred, dressed in a wild display of sixties attire, introduced himself as Sergeant Pepperz, with a Z. He had an uncanny resemblance to John Lennon, wire-rimmed glasses and all.

"Welcome ladies and gents. I'm your guide on this magical, mystery tour through historic Boston. I'll dole out lots of little-known facts and we'll have a groovy time. But first I need you all to practice your duck call. I see by the blank looks that you aren't familiar with our duck call. What do ducks say?"

Anne and Patrick glanced at each other. Someone from the back shouted, "Quack."

Sergeant Pepperz pumped his hand in the air. "Exactly. Let me hear everyone. On the count of three. One, two, three."

"Quack!" Anne lifted her voice. She nudged Patrick in the ribs. "Come on say *quack*."

"Quack," he repeated dryly.

She laughed and turned her attention back to the conductor.

"When we pass through an intersection, I'll blow my whistle and you all respond with a resounding quack. And when we pass another duck tour, we quack. And when we pass a police officer, we quack."

"You think this is silly, don't you?" Anne remarked.

"When I was six it was fun. Now, not so much."

She shook her head. "What do you do for fun?"

He took off his glasses and began to clean them with a cloth from his pocket. "I write."

"That book is done, right? Are you working on another?"

"I have a few short stories," he replied, keeping his gaze averted.

She didn't understand why he'd be self-conscious about his work. "I'd love to read them."

He slipped his glasses back on. "I wouldn't want to bother you."

Laying a light touch on his arm, she said, "It wouldn't be a bother."

The amphibious beast began to move. "This is so cool," she exclaimed

"I'm glad you're enjoying yourself," he replied.

Anne searched his expression trying to determine if he were enjoying their time together. The man was a mystery. A source of conflict and complication. She really shouldn't be with him now, except she didn't want to be alone, either. She was tired of being along.

He looked composed and attentive, which made her all that more curious about his reaction in church earlier that morning.

"Did you enjoy the service this morning before your asthma attack?" she asked, watching closely to gage his reaction. She didn't really think he'd had an asthma attack, but something sure had gotten to him.

He shrugged. "It was fine."

"I thought the message was a good one, focusing on God's faithfulness through troubled times." She certainly could attest to that.

Without God, she probably wouldn't still be alive. He'd proved Himself to her.

His jaw tensed. "I suppose. But I'm not so sure that faith is all it's cracked up to be."

Curious, she stared at him. "Why would you say that?"

"Because faith doesn't change anything. Not really. People can pray until they're blue in the face but what good does it do? Is evil wiped out? Are the problems of this world taken away? No. So why bother?"

His jaded take on faith left her feeling very sad for him. Something or someone had set him against God. Maybe a prayer not answered in the way he wanted or in the time frame he wanted? She reached out and touched his hand. "I'm sorry you're hurting."

He slipped his hand away. "I'm not hurting." He pointed to a structure on their left. "Here's Trinity Church."

The vehicle rumbled past the beautifully constructed building, and though Anne oohed and ahhed over the architecture as their conductor gave a brief history of the church that dated back to 1733, she couldn't help the sadness settling in her soul for Patrick.

He tapped her shoulder and pointed at the botanical gardens that were coming up. She clapped her hands when she saw the beautifully crafted swan boats full of tourists gliding through the man-made lake.

They continued on through the streets of Boston, taking in the many sights. Soon they were heading down a little incline straight into the Charles River.

Anne laughed with glee and was thankful the lunch they'd shared before the tour had been light. She'd hate to be caught with a bout of motion sickness in front of Patrick.

She glanced back toward the shore from which they'd come and her gaze landed on a man sitting in the very back of the boat.

Her breath stalled in her lungs. Cam, the Asian man from the college, sat three rows back.

FIVE

Anne quickly jerked around to sit forward. Her whole body tensed.

"Patrick. Is that Cam in the back of the boat?"

"What?" He turned his head to look. He shrugged as he returned his gaze to her. "I don't know. Could be."

"Why is he here?" Her uneasiness crept along the length of her spine beneath the suddenly overwarm suit.

"Taking the tour?"

"Do you think he followed us?" She fought back a fisson of panic.

"Are you all right? You've gone awfully pale," Patrick said, his voice low and concerned.

"I want off this boat."

Patrick took her shaky hands, his touch solid and secure. She tightened her hold on him.

"Tell me what has you so spooked."

How did she tell him she had a creepy feeling about

his would-be student? Had he been the one to vandal-ize her car and was now stalking her? Was this all to do with what had happened in Atlantic City or not?

She decided to confide some of her fear to Patrick. She really needed a shoulder to lean on, but couldn't allow herself anything more than a superficial support. She was tired of being alone and scared. "It just seems odd that Cam came to your office, and then my car was vandalized, and now he's here on this tour with us."

Patrick's brow furrowed. "I'll be right back."

Before Anne could protest, Patrick got up and moved toward the back.

Anne shifted in her seat to watch Patrick talking to Cam. She couldn't hear their conversation but she could see Cam shaking his head and introducing Patrick to the girl sitting at his side.

Anne adjusted her view to see a beautiful Asian woman she hadn't noticed before. Patrick shook Cam's hand before returning to his seat.

"Sir, I'm going to have to ask you to stay seated," called the conductor.

Patrick acknowledged the sergeant with a wave then turned to Anne. "He and his sister are taking the tour. She's here visiting. There's nothing sinister going on."

Heat stole into her cheeks. "Oh. Still…what are the odds that they'd take the same tour we are?"

"Is there something you're not telling me?"

There were a lot of things. Things she couldn't fully confide to him no matter how much she enjoyed his company. Or that affection for him had taken root in her heart.

She was becoming attached and wishing she could lean on him. Spending the day with him had obviously been a mistake.

One she would have to be careful not to repeat.

"I overreacted. The big city and all. Back home we always heard stories of how dangerous cities could be. I guess somewhere in my brain that belief was ingrained."

He looked puzzled. "I thought you said you were from L.A.?"

Uh-oh. "Yes, sort of," she hedged. "A small town. You know there's tons of them on the outskirts. The suburbs." She quickly adjusted her focus outside the boat to the ramp coming up. "Here we go."

The vehicle made a smooth transition back to land. She chatted nonstop about the sights coming into view. Bunker Hill, the *USS Constitution*, the famous bar used in the opening credits of the TV show *Cheers*.

If Patrick was bothered by her jabbering or her inconsistent disclosure about her life she certainly wasn't going to give him a chance to comment.

When the tour was over, Anne kept a running commentary going on all they'd seen as they left the city and headed back to Newton and her apartment building.

He parked the car and walked around just as she opened the passenger door. She took his offered hand, aware of how well their hands fit together. "Thank you for everything."

"You're welcome. May I walk you up?"

Uncertainty lanced through her. There were so many reasons why she should say no. Distaste from the lingering image of the dead rat, her paranoia on the tour, the way her heart beat by fits and starts every time he was close.

But what harm could come from him walking her to her door?

Maybe a kiss?

The thought sent her already volatile pulse boomeranging through her veins.

She really should say no. Her gaze drifted to his mouth. "Yes, you may."

He followed her up the stairs to the fourth floor. At her door, she halted and tried to steady her breath. "Again, thank you."

"It's been a while since we ate. How about we order a pizza?"

The request was unexpected and way too pleasant. "You want to stay? For dinner?"

Mentally picturing the room behind her and trying to recall if she'd picked up her clothes from the night before, Anne remained still. Her breakfast dishes still lay in the sink. When was the last time she'd cleaned the bathroom?

Patrick stepped back. "I've overstepped myself."

"No, no. It's just…" Her life was a disaster. What did it matter if he discovered she wasn't the world's best housekeeper? She wasn't trying to impress him. She should be protecting him from herself, her past, but…

She pushed open the door. "I apologize now for the mess."

Princess let out a loud meow and her tail swished. She regarded Patrick with distain before prancing over to her dish and meowing again.

"Her dinner's late," Anne explained as she shut the door behind them and out of habit threw the bolt into place. Turning back to Patrick, the room she'd lived in for these past three months seemed to have shrunk.

"You feed her and I'll order the pizza," he said.

He moved purposely toward the cordless phone on the scarred old oak coffee table in front of the worn plaid upholstered love seat, her only seating except for the two cane-back chairs pushed up to the small, round dinette table in the corner.

Anne paused on the way to the cupboard. She had a refrigerator full of food. "Would you mind if we don't order out? I'll fix a salad and garlic bread."

Midstride, he pivoted toward her. His long legs carried him to her side in just a few steps. "Not at all. I'll help."

The little kitchen space barely accommodated her let alone his larger masculine frame. She squeezed past him and bent down to fill Princess's bowl. "No, that's okay. You're the guest."

"Self-invited."

She straightened, pivoted and bumped against him. Every nerve ending shimmied like a firefly's dance. "I'm glad you stayed," she said, hoping to relieve any regret he might have for asking to.

Through the lenses of his glasses, his deep mocha-colored eyes were unreadable. His gaze dropped to her mouth. She moistened her lips, which was pretty difficult considering how dry her mouth had gone.

"What would you like me to do?"

His softly spoken words sent suggestions cascading through her brain.

Kiss me.

Hold me.

Love me.

She bit down hard on the inside of her cheek to trap the ridiculous words from escaping as her mind scrambled to clear her thoughts.

No. No. No. She didn't want him to kiss or hold her. Well...okay, maybe she did just the tiniest bit, but she certainly wasn't looking for love.

Her life was too unsettled and unpredictable.

Don't get attached.

It was good advice. She had to remember it.

She stepped back, her foot landing on Princess's tail. The cat screeched. Anne jumped.

Patrick raised an eyebrow. A interested gleam in those fabulous, chocolate-brown eyes. "A little edgy?"

She could almost taste chocolate melting on her tongue. She made a noise to affirm his statement and to banish the imagined sensation of rich cocoa.

He rubbed his hands together. "Should I get started on the bread or the salad?"

Bread?

Salad?

"Oh, right." Dinner. He'd been asking how he could

help, not…what she'd thought. She wasn't sure if she was relieved or disappointed.

"It'd be great if you'd tackle the bread."

She brushed past him to grab the loaf of sourdough sitting in the fruit basket. "There's a knife—"

She turned and he was there again, inches from her. She inhaled the lingering aroma of his aftershave that now mingled with his musky, masculine scent. She stifled a sigh and resisted the urge to rub her cheek against his like a cat looking for affection.

Pushing the loaf of bread into his chest until he stepped back, she continued, "Let me get the knife."

From a small drawer she retrieved the serrated bread knife, then slid open the cutting board, effectively trapping herself between the stove and oven, the cutting board and him. He took the knife and laid it on the cutting board next to the bread while he slipped out of his jacket. His white dress shirt fit attractively against his wide shoulders and lean torso.

She turned away and set the oven to broil. From the cupboard behind her, she took out garlic powder and set it in the cutting board. She was able to open the re-frigerator door wide enough to grab a stick of butter and the salad fixings, plus the cold cooked chicken she'd picked up the night before. Making do with the small amount of counter space between the sink and the stove, she prepared their salad.

They worked in silence, the rasp of the bread knife filling the kitchen in tempo to the chopping of her paring knife as she cut vegetables. The unfamiliarity of the domestic scene started a low hum of yearning in her soul.

Her father had never helped in the kitchen. That had always been "the woman's" place to him. Anne tried to recall ever jointly making a meal with any of her ex-boyfriends. She couldn't.

Takeout or microwavable had been the norm until recently. Ever since she'd moved to Boston, knowing that everything in her life was going to change.

Witnessing a murder had a way of doing that.

When the salad bowl was filled, he stepped aside so she could set the bowl on the table. Patrick put the bread in the oven. A few minutes later, with their bread toasted and their salads served, they sat at the round table.

His long legs tangled with hers for a moment before they settled into comfortable positions. At first, Anne tried to keep her knee from resting against his leg, but soon she relaxed and enjoyed the warmth.

"Did you mean it?"

Anne chewed a tomato she'd just popped into her mouth. The acidic fruit burst with flavor. She swallowed. "Mean what?"

Patrick weighed his words. "That you liked my book."

A smile tugged at the corner of her mouth. She leaned forward for emphasis. "Yes. Very much so. That's why I printed it because I got so caught up in the story that I'm sure I missed some things that needed to be fixed."

The bemused expression on his handsome face was endearing. "You didn't throw it away did you?" she asked.

A muscle in his cheek twitched, but his mouth didn't. "The printout, yes, but the file is still on my computer."

"Have you sent it out to any publishers?"

"No."

The reply came out quickly and in a tone that conveyed the very idea was preposterous.

"Chicken," she teased.

His eyes darkened and not with amusement. "You're the only person who even knows about the book, let alone has read it."

And both by default and without his permission.

She instantly sobered. "Which begs the question why? Why would you keep a talent like yours hidden?"

"It's private."

"The answer to my question is private or the whole subject is private?"

He thought. "Both."

Considering she had enough issues in her own life that she deemed private, she could understand, even respect his answer. But that didn't mean she agreed with the keeping of secrets. And for some irrational reason she wished for there to be truth between them. At least on some level.

"Do you enjoy jazz music?"

Thrown by the abrupt change in topic, she had to think a minute. "You mean music with saxophones and breathy vocals?"

Patrick's mouth quirked upward. "Yeah, something like that."

"Yes. I think so. Why?"

"I have tickets to a jazz concert tomorrow night. Would you like to join me?"

Unexpected warmth at his request spread through her chest. "I would. Thank you."

The pleasure in his gaze touched her like a caress. "Great," he said.

A tingle of excitement lit her senses and caused her heart to thud against her ribs in an erratic beat. Her gaze dropped to her plate. She'd just accepted an official date with the professor.

So much for keeping her distance.

Scullers Jazz Club on Soldier Road in downtown Boston overlooked the Charles River and showcased the Boston skyline with huge floor-to-ceiling windows. Rich mahogany walls, intimate seating for small parties and a stage with a lush red curtain backdrop created an ambiance few clubs in Boston could compete with. Patrick liked its cozy, less crowded atmosphere. And tonight was the first time he'd ever brought a woman here with him. He hadn't ever wanted to share this very personal passion for jazz with one before. Doing so now was a bit unnerving.

A brunette hostess showed Patrick and Anne to a table near a window where they could enjoy the view as well as the stage.

"This is lovely," Anne remarked as she sat in the chair Patrick pulled out for her.

He took his seat. "Scullers has the best jazz in town."

She picked up the menu but didn't open it. "Do you come here often?"

"Yes, depending on who's playing."

"I wouldn't have pictured you as a jazz fan—more of a classical kind of guy."

"I'm full of surprises," he quipped, enjoying how beautiful she looked tonight with her normally spiked hair a bit softer somehow. Though she still wore the baggy brown dress suit she'd worn to work that day, in the soft ambient light, the brown complemented her complexion in a way it didn't in the harsher fluorescent lights of the college.

She smiled. "Yes, you are full of surprises." She opened the menu. "What would you suggest?"

"The tenderloin over mashed garlic potatoes," he said decisively.

She shut the menu. "Sounds good."

For a moment silence stretched between them.

"Have you seen any good movies lately?" Anne asked.

Grateful that she'd started the small talk with something easy, he told her about a foreign film he'd watched recently.

"You speak French?" she asked.

"No. The movie had subtitles."

She looked impressed. "I've never watched a film with subtitles. Is it hard to follow?"

"You get used to it."

The waiter came over and they ordered their meals. The conversation strayed to books.

"I read Christian romance novels," she announced.

He knew what romance novels were but Christian ones? He'd bet his mother would like them, if she hadn't already discovered them. He'd have to ask her. "I didn't know there was such a thing. I read more literary works, myself. I want to be challenged, provoked to think."

She leaned forward, her expression showing earnest interest. "Don't you ever read just to enjoy the story? Most of the literary books I've tried are sad and depressing. Wouldn't you rather read more uplifting and hopeful books?"

"Well, I do read—" he couldn't believe he was going to confess this to her "—horror, for pleasure."

She blinked "*Horror?* You find that pleasurable?

"Okay, maybe pleasurable isn't the right word. But they keep my interest."

She made a face. "I've read a few and couldn't sleep for weeks."

A mental image played across his mind of Anne curled up on a couch engrossed in a novel and biting one nail as she turned the pages. She'd be so cute, needing someone to comfort her from the scary story. He shook away the image.

"To each his own, I guess," he replied and silently told himself to get a grip. Just because they were out now and the evening was going nicely, didn't mean he should be thinking about spending more time with her. It wasn't like they were dating with marriage in mind. This was just two people out for a little dinner and music. Nothing more.

"I suppose." She gazed past his shoulder, her eyebrows drawing together.

He turned to see what made her frown. "What's wrong?"

Her expression cleared. "Nothing." She shook her head, clearly embarrassed. "I thought I saw Cam again, but I was mistaken."

"He sure bugged you, didn't he?"

"I think the vandalism to my car unnerved me more than I'd thought."

Protectiveness seared through him. He reached across the table and took her hand. The warm, soft skin felt so good within his grasp. "Your reaction is understandable."

She flexed her fingers around his. "Thanks."

The waiter interrupted. "Here we go, two tenderloin dinners."

Reluctantly letting go of her, Patrick sat back and tried to focus on the savory food.

During their meal they chatted about sports and playfully argued over who would win the upcoming World Series. When their meal was devoured and their plates cleared away, Patrick used the excuse of improving his angle toward the stage to scoot his chair closer to Anne.

An excited buzz filled the air when the MC stepped to centerstage and introduced the musicians.

For the next hour, they were treated to some amazing jazz and Patrick reveled in the music as much as watching the play of emotions dancing across Anne's face.

When the last song ended, they stood to clap along with the other patrons.

"That was wonderful," she exclaimed. As they left the club and walked to his car, she added, "Thank you for inviting me."

"You're welcome." He was glad to know she enjoyed herself. He really relished her company, and delighted in the easy way they talked without awkwardness.

When they reached his car, he held open the passenger door. For a moment Anne seemed frozen, her gaze on a Hispanic man standing in the shadows near a closed store.

"Anne?"

She wrenched her gaze back to him. Her whole body shuddered. "I'm sorry. I don't know what's the matter with me. I keep freaking myself out."

Once she was settled in the seat, he leaned in close. "I'm not going to let anything happen to you, okay?"

Though she nodded, anxiety lingered in her violet colored gaze. She didn't believe him Why?

Was she really only paranoid because of the car break-in or was there something else she wasn't saying?

And how did he get her to trust him enough to tell him?

"Would you like to come in for coffee?" Anne asked, not wanting the evening to end. She'd thoroughly enjoyed herself, regardless of her minipanic attacks. First imagining she'd seen Cam in the crowd and then later thinking the man on the street was staring at her. She really had to get a grip or Patrick would think she was certifiable.

"Coffee would be great," he replied as he walked with her to the door of her apartment building.

Once inside her apartment, Patrick took a seat at the dining room table and she set the decaf coffee to brewing. She pulled out some scones she'd picked up earlier in the day from the bakery at the end of the street. Putting them on a tray, she turned on the oven to warm the pastries up.

The phone rang, the sound jangled along Anne's nerves.

She stared at the instrument. Only a very small, select few had this number. She didn't even have an answering machine because there was no point.

"Are you going to answer?" Patrick asked after the fifth ring.

Meeting his quizzical gaze, she stood. "Yes. Of course."

If she didn't answer, Patrick would ask questions. Questions she wasn't at liberty to answer. Though spilling her guts to him was very tempting. She could really use a voice of reason to keep the nightmares at bay.

She moved across the room and lifted the handset from its cradle.

Before pressing Talk she took a bracing breath. "Hello?"

Heavy breathing met her greeting.

She let loose a disgusted noise in her throat and clicked the end button.

"Problem?" Patrick had risen. Concern etched lines in his face.

"Crank call." She set the device back in its base. "Probably bored teens. I can remember doing stuff like that. We'd randomly dial and then usually make some dumb joke, like did you know your refrigerator was running? You better hurry before it gets away."

"So you were a bit of a troublemaker, eh?" He raised an eyebrow.

She couldn't tell if he was teasing her or simply stating the obvious. "You could say that."

"Where are your parents?"

"Back home."

"What brought you out here?"

She didn't like the bend in the road this conversation was taking. "You know, I have a friend in the publishing industry. I could send him your book. Get some feedback."

He held up his hand. "No way."

She didn't understand why he'd refuse. Why write something if you didn't want to see it published?

The phone rang again. With a jerk, she grabbed the receiver and punched the talk button. "Yes?"

More heavy breathing.

Anne's jaw tightened in annoyance. "Listen, you. This isn't funny." She clicked End without waiting for a reply.

Keeping the phone in her hand, she moved to the kitchen area and set the phone on the counter.

Patrick stacked the dishes on the rack by the sink. "You could always have your number changed."

She sighed. "I'm sure it's just kids."

She didn't need anymore changes. And if it wasn't kids calling, she'd have bigger problems than changing her phone number to deal with.

When the phone ran for the third time, she picked up before the second ring. "Yes." Resignation laced her voice.

A dry chuckle that sounded anything but teenaged made the hairs on her arms raise. Then a voice, dark and dangerous whispered in her ear. "Have you ever heard the scream of a dying rat?"

Fear rammed into her skull, rendering her speechless. Anne fought back smothering panic as the world receded into a pinpoint where only Patrick's face kept her sanity intact.

The voice, so wicked and close, continued, "It's very satisfying."

The dark night air was just warm enough for people to leave their windows cracked opened. A boon for the man dressed in black as he slid the bottom floor window up just far enough to slip through. He didn't worry about prints. His soft leather gloves wouldn't leave any. Blending into the shadowed interior, he made his way toward the door underneath which a beam of light threw just enough glow to navigate the room's furnishings.

Cautiously he cracked the door and peered into the hall. The dull overhead lights illuminated the empty corridor. Making his way silently through the building to the door of his target, his breathing slowed in preparation for entering the apartment.

He took out his tools and used them on the apartment's lock. Before opening the door, he unscrewed the hall lights so there'd be no change in shadows when the door swung forward. Once inside the apartment, he slinked toward the bedroom, having already assessed the apartment during the day when the target hadn't been home. He moved to where he knew his prize awaited.

A figure slept under the cover of a sheet. The man swiftly placed his hand over her mouth as she jerked awake. Her hands flayed the air and her feet kicked. From the sheath at his side he pulled out a large knife. The woman clawed at his gloved hands.

He leaned in close. "You should have kept your mouth shut."

With one clean arc, the man sliced through the woman's throat and her fighting ended.

SIX

The squad room door burst open.

Glad for the interruption, Lidia jerked her gaze from the case file in front of her. She'd been working a double domestic homicide that looked open and shut. The teenage son amped up on meth had shot both parents with the father's hunting rifle.

The kid had passed out afterward and didn't remember a thing. Not unheard of, but the weapon had been wiped clean.

Which was odd. Odd enough to make Lidia suspect there had been another person involved.

Rick, unusually harried, came straight to Lidia's desk. "We've got a situation."

"Yes, we do." She tapped the file.

"Not that. On the Domingo case," he stated, agitation clouding his eyes and edging his tone.

Lidia's lungs slammed against her ribs, trapping her breath. "Tell me."

"One of our witnesses has turned up dead."

Please no. Oh Lord, please not Anne.

She swallowed a shudder of pure dread. She never should have let herself become emotionally involved with a witness, but the young woman had struck a latent parental instinct Lidia had been helpless to deny. "Details."

Rick laid out a series of photographs. No words were needed.

Lidia closed her eyes.

Such a waste.

Patrick watched the color drain from Anne's face and her body go rigid. Her violet eyes glazed over with shock from whatever she'd just heard. Something was wrong. He took the receiver from her slackened fingers and put it to his ear. Dial tone. He clicked off and set the phone aside before taking Anne by the hands and leading her to the love seat.

"Anne," he said softly.

Her gaze shifted slightly toward him. She blinked several times. Her body did one long shudder and her eyes cleared.

"What was that?" he asked.

Her color returned but the tight lines around her mouth spoke of how disturbing she found the call. "Just another prank."

He didn't believe that just a prank call could upset her so badly. "Tell me what was said."

She shook her head. "It's late. You should go." She stood abruptly.

Whoa, what had her so spooked? Whatever it was, he didn't want to leave her like this. She'd started to relax during dinner. He still could hardly fathom her praise of his writing. But now she was distressed again and trying not to keep her emotions from showing.

"You're upset. You shouldn't be alone. Is there someone you can call to come stay with you or somewhere you could go?"

Two little lines appeared between her eyebrows. "No. I'm fine. I'll be fine." She moved restlessly into the kitchen, wiping down the counters.

Concern arced through him. But he couldn't stay with her. There was only the one Murphy bed and not even a sofa, just the love seat that had seen better days.

In fact, so much of the furniture in the small studio had seen better days. It looked like she'd shopped at the local thrift store. He suddenly realized there were no personal items or photos or anything that gave him insight to Anne.

He didn't feel like he really knew her and thinking about it, she'd been very close-mouthed about her past. Why?

She stopped moving and stared at him expectantly. There was no other option than to do as she'd asked.

But that didn't mean he was going to abandon her. It wasn't in his nature.

As soon as the door closed behind Patrick, Anne rushed to her purse and dug out her cell phone. Somehow, someway, her location had been compromised. And clearly the car vandalism *hadn't* been random.

She speed-dialed the only person she trusted but voice mail picked up. Unsure what to make of that, she tried to keep the panic at bay as she left a message.

There was one other number she could call. Scrolling through the cell's phonebook, she found the number she needed.

A man answered on the second ring. "Klein."

"This is Anne Johnson."

"Hold."

The line went quiet.

The adrenaline that had pumped through her veins after the initial shock from the call now slowly drained, leaving her weakened. She sank onto the love seat, pulling her knees to her chest. Princess jumped onto the cushion beside her and let out a loud meow before rubbing her head against Anne's updrawn legs.

Taking comfort in the cat, Anne tried not to let her mind dwell on the sinister words still echoing inside her head.

Being summoned so commandingly to the D.A.'s office put Lidia in a bad mood. She stepped into the outer office just as Jane was hanging up the phone.

Jane grimaced. "You can go in, but he's in a foul mood."

Lidia snorted. "So am I."

She pushed open the door and entered. Porter stood facing the window. "How could you let this happen?"

Lidia stopped short. "Excuse me?"

Porter turned and glared at her before taking his seat behind his desk. Fatigue or stress darkened the skin around his eyes. "You said you had the witnesses secure. Now we've lost one."

Holding on to her patience, Lidia planted her hands on the D.A.'s desk and leaned forward. "First, you don't order me to your office like some flunky law clerk and then snap at me. Second, I told you one witness was in hiding and refused our protection. That witness has paid a stiff price."

And though she had her own methods of keeping tabs on those involved in the investigation, she added, "Third, if you want to know about the other two key witnesses you should be talking to the U.S. Marshals assigned to their cases."

He rubbed a hand over his jaw. "You're right. I'm sorry. This case is falling apart."

Remembering the cryptic message shc'd received late last night from Anne had taken a chunk out her confidence, but she had to hope for the best. Had to trust that God would see this through. "This case is solid even without the one witness."

He shook his head, his troubled gaze meeting hers. "The video placing Domingo in the hotel has disappeared."

Feeling as if she'd just been rammed in the gut with a night stick, she sank into a chair. "How?"

His mouth pressed into a thin, angry line. "Honestly I think we have a leak somewhere in the system."

Lidia digested that information. If someone had access to the evidence, they could realistically gain access to the case files. "We have to warn the marshals. All the witnesses could be compromised."

Porter sighed with resignation. "It's already happened."

The bottom fell out of Lidia's soul. She prepared herself for the worst. "Tell me."

Abandoning a woman to her fate might not be in Patrick's "nature," but he certainly wasn't built for an overnight vigil of Anne's apartment while crammed inside the Mini Cooper.

The sun was just peeking over the horizon. Cold and stiff, Patrick rolled his shoulders and checked his watch. Nearly six. Anne probably wouldn't come out for at least another hour. He contemplated walking down to the café at the corner. He could really use some coffee. Instead he leaned his head back.

A knock at his window startled him awake. He hadn't meant to sleep. He bolted upright, bruising his knees on the steering wheel and bumping his head on the roof.

At the window beside him stood Anne. All in one piece and smiling. A welcome sight. Her gray business suit hung off her slim frame and gaped at the sides where she bent slightly to look in at him.

He rolled down the window. "Morning."

"Hi. What are you doing?"

"Waiting for you."

Her eyebrows rose. "Have you been here all night?"

"Yes," he admitted.

"Wow," she said, her voice and expression both incredulous.

Not sure he could get out and then back in, he said, "Hop in. I'll drive you to the college."

As she came around to the passenger side, Patrick's gaze scanned the street and sidewalk. People starting their Monday morning.

A man with a dog came out of the building next to Anne's. The dog, a big mastiff, pulled at his leash, nearly dragging the poor guy off his feet. Shouldn't have something you can't control, Patrick thought.

The man and dog passed another man who stood slightly turned away. Something about the wiry, dark-haired fellow struck a chord in Patrick. He couldn't make out the man's features because he had a Red Sox's hat pulled low over his eyes.

Anne slid into the seat. "I can't believe you slept in your car all night."

Keeping an eye on the man, Patrick started the engine and turned the heat to full-blast. Cold air flew at him from the vents, but as the car rolled down the street and picked up speed, the night's claim on the car receded and warmth filled the interior. "It was a bit uncomfortable."

She touched his arm. "I'll bet. Especially for a guy your size."

The unexpected tender gestured tightened his chest and drew his attention. "I didn't expect you for another hour or so."

Her hand slipped away, leaving in its place a warmed spot. "I started out early enough to familiarize myself with the transit train and then the bus," she explained while she held both hands up to the heat vent.

Patrick's gaze searched the rearview mirror for the dark haired man. He was gone. "Makes sense. But I said I would give you a ride."

"You don't have to chauffeur me around, you know."

"I don't mind." He checked the rearview mirror ,again. A green American made car pulled out behind them. Two men with sunglasses sat in the front seat.

"You have your own life. I don't want to be a burden," she stated.

The car stayed behind them for several blocks. "You're not a burden."

She sat quietly for a moment as if trying to comprehend his words. "The body shop said I'd have my car back in a few days."

"Great." When he turned to get on the road that would take him to the college, the car didn't take the on ramp. "Then for the next few days, I'm your guy. I mean your driver."

Pink bloomed in her cheeks, mirroring the heat he felt creeping up his neck at his own fumbling.

"Really, Patrick, you don't have to."

He glanced at her. "Do you *not* want me to?"

The troubled expression in her eyes tore at him. "It's not that. I just feel bad, like I'm inconveniencing you."

"If I were inconvenienced I wouldn't offer. But if you would rather I back off, I will."

"No, actually, I wouldn't."

He glanced over at her again, searching her gaze, hoping she wasn't just being polite, but the sincerity in her expression tugged a small smile from him. "Good."

They drove in silence for a moment. When he checked his rearview again, he couldn't be sure but he thought he saw the same American made car three cars back. He chastised himself for being overly suspicious. There were a million of the same make and model all over the place. There was no reason he should suspect they were being followed.

He could feel Anne's gaze assessing him.

"Where do you live?" she asked.

"Not far from BC." He maneuvered around a slow-moving delivery truck.

"We could stop so you can freshen up and change."

He cast a brief look her way, surprised by her words. "That's okay."

"No, it's not." She waved a hand to emphasize her words. "Look at you. You're a mess."

Because of her teasing tone, he didn't take offense with her assessment. He felt like a mess. "Gee, thanks," he teased.

She worried her bottom lip for a moment. "I don't mean to insult you, but this isn't you. You can't go into work like this."

With a shrug, he replied, "It doesn't matter."

"What will people say?"

Her affronted tone made him pause and chance a curious glance at her. "I don't know. Should I care?"

Her eyes grew big. "Yes. You've a reputation to maintain. You're an associate professor. You can't show up to the college looking like you slept in your car."

Her concern sent pleasure rippling through his system. "But I did sleep in my car."

"Which begs the question why?" She turned in her seat to fully face him. "Why did you sleep outside my apartment?"

An odd sense of self-consciousness attacked him. How did he reason out the need to protect her, even to himself? With the truth? He didn't really have much choice. "You were pretty upset last night. I wanted to make sure you were safe and to be here if you needed anything."

The affection in her expression made him swallow quickly.

"Really? That's so sweet." She touched his arm again, her hand pale and delicate against his tweed coat. "I mean, I don't think I've ever had anyone do anything so nice for me before."

He liked how her words made him feel approved of and appreciated. "It's not that big a deal."

She tightened her hand, her fingers firm on his arm. "Yes, it is. To me, it is."

Keeping one hand on the wheel, he covered her hand with his own. The contact melted him inside. "Thanks."

"For what?"

He lifted her hand and brought her knuckles to his lips to place a featherlight kiss there. "For making me feel so good."

"How'd…how'd I do that?"

"Just by being you."

Her gaze dropped and she slipped her hand away. Her withdrawal sent disappointment curling through his heart. He had the distinct impression that he'd somehow upset her with his words.

Now why would that be?

A stone wall encapsulated the many buildings of Patrick's apartment complex. As they drove through the parking lot, Anne caught a glimpse of a pool surrounded by a wide concrete patio with several lawn chairs and sets of tables with chairs.

Patrick parked near the entrance to the third building. She followed him into the entryway which was tiled with gray stone and the walls were textured in rich tones of blue and cream.

The elevator was mirrored and soothing classical music played from speakers concealed in the ceiling. They exited on to the top floor.

Patrick led her to the twentieth apartment near the opposite end of the building.

He unlocked his door and pushed it open. "Welcome."

She stepped over the threshold into a stylized dwelling that could have easily been a feature for a modern living type of magazine. To the left of the front door was the kitchen that sported sand-colored granite counters, white appliances and a beige flecked tile floor. To the right she glimpsed the powder room with the same flooring, white fixtures and ecru colored hand towels.

The living space had a cream carpet. Lots of cream carpeting and cream walls. A light brown leather sectional dominated the middle of the room and faced a beige-toned stone hearth fireplace. A round pine table and four matching chairs sat near the wall beside a light, finished shelf system with a high-tech sound equipment. "It's…uh." Very vanilla. With caramel sauce. "Very nice."

"Thanks. I'm comfortable here."

Her gaze was drawn to the only bit of bright color in the main living quarters of the apartment. A display of photos in pine shadow boxes lined a wall. She went to inspect the images. "Is this your family?"

He came to stand beside her. "Yes." He pointed to a ruggedly handsome, smiling man with his arm slung around a beautiful, laughing redhead. "That's my brother Brody and his wife, Kate. They're expecting their first child around Christmas. He's a sheriff in Havensport, on Nantucket."

Patrick motioned to a picture of a young woman with curly dark hair holding a bouquet of red roses. Her serene smile and kind eyes seemed to stare straight at Anne.

"This is Megan, my sister. She lives in New York

City and runs a trendy art gallery. Not long after our father was killed she came down with a bad case of strep, which triggered OCD. The doctor's said because her immune system was weakened from grief, she became susceptible to the disorder. "

Empathy played a sad melody through Anne's heart. "That must be hard on her."

"It is, but she's coping." He tapped the next picture. "And this is the baby, Ryan." Patrick walked away from the wall toward the kitchen. "Would you care for some coffee?"

"Please."

The man in the photo had a roguish gleam in his dark eyes that was far from infantile. "What does Ryan do?"

"He's an investment broker," he said as he made the coffee. "And very successful for how young he is but he's always been that way. Once scheme after another, trying to make his fortune. I have to admit his entrepreneurial spirit has served him well over the years. He'd set up lemonade stands at the park across from our home and rake in enough cash to pay for us all to go to the movies every Saturday night."

"So he doesn't hoard his cash?"

Patrick gave an equivocal gesture with his hand. "Yes and no. He's generous but smart. He'll be set for life by the time he's fifty, yet…"

"Yet?"

"I worry that he'll miss out on living if he stays so focused on accumulating wealth."

His concern for Ryan endeared him to her. She wished she and her siblings had been as close-knit.

The last portrait was of an older couple. Patrick's parents. "Your mother is stunning."

Patrick set a mug on the counter for her. "Yes, she is. That picture was taken the year before my father was killed."

His words, stated so matter-of-factly, curled around her heart and squeezed. Flashes of his novel came back to her. A deep, penetrating sadness welled inside, blurring her vision.

Keeping her voice even, she asked, "How did he die?"

When he didn't immediately answer, she turned to find him watching her with the oddest expression she couldn't decipher.

"I'm sorry. I shouldn't pry."

He gave his head a quick shake as if to clear his thoughts and then picked up his mug of coffee but didn't take a drink, just stared into the dark liquid. "In the line of duty. Sort of."

He glanced up. In the depth of his eyes she saw his hurt and anger, but then it was quickly banked by his normal stoic expression.

"He'd picked Brody up from school late one afternoon. On their way home a call came over the radio. Dad responded."

He couldn't have said what she thought she just heard. "With your brother in the car?"

"Yes."

Empathy and anger roared through her. Tears burned the back of her eyes. "How old was your brother?"

"Twelve."

She looked back at the photos, giving herself a moment to clear the clogged tears from her throat.

"Dad was all about duty and honor. I think he thought he was invincible. He left Brody in the car while he went into the situation."

Her stomach lurched. "Did Brody stay in the car?"

There was no mistaking the spurt of rage in his eyes before he blinked it away. "No. He saw my father die."

Images streaked across her brain. The remembered noises, the smells. The horror. She couldn't imagine a child witnessing a murder. Witnessing the death of a parent. She ached for this family that was torn apart by tragedy.

"How awful," she whispered, wishing there were words to express her sympathy.

He briefly closed his eyes. When he opened them the remoteness in his gaze left her breathless. "It was awful. For all of us."

"You said Brody is a sheriff."

He gulped from his mug before answering. "That's right."

"Amazing that he'd choose law enforcement."

"I think he still wants justice for our father's murder."

Her breath hitched. "They never caught the guy?"

"No. There were no witnesses. Brody only saw the man's back as he ran away."

If Anne ever had a doubt about the path she'd chosen, to testify rather than take Jean Luc's money and disappear, those doubts had just been laid to rest.

Someone had to stand up for the rights of the victim. Someone had to bring the criminal to justice. For Jean Luc, that someone was Anne.

Too bad someone hadn't been able to do that for the McClain family.

She wanted to wrap Patrick in her embrace and somehow, someway heal the wound so evident in Patrick's heart.

But she didn't believe she had that power.

She didn't believe Patrick would let her. So all she could do was say a silent prayer that God would bring this hurting man peace.

SEVEN

Patrick made his way across campus back to Carney Hall where Anne was now helping the English department with their computers. He hadn't liked leaving her there, but logically knew she'd be fine. There was no reason for him to be feeling like he needed to stick by her all day.

Even so, he just couldn't erase the fear he'd seen in her eyes last night after that phone call.

This morning she'd seemed calm and hadn't said a word about the call. Instead she'd been very interested in his family.

Talking about his father's death still hurt even after all these years but he'd become good at controlling the pain. He was sure Anne had no idea how hard it had been to answer her questions.

As he approached the building, he glanced toward the public parking lot. He paused as his gaze landed on a familiar car. Near the end of the last row, there was a car matching the one that had followed them earlier this morning.

Patrick's gaze searched the grounds, taking in the smattering of students and faculty.

Patrick noticed a man in a gray business suit wearing sunglasses step from around the corner of the building and ascend the stairs into Carney Hall.

Wait a sec! An image of the car with the two men in sunglasses flashed through his mind.

Coincidence? Not likely.

He rushed inside and took the stairs to the fourth floor two at a time. Business suit guy leaned against the wall just outside the office where Anne worked.

He'd taken off his sunglasses, his face smooth, young. A student who'd taken a fancy to Anne? In a business suit? No way. There was something strange about the man.

"Hey." Patrick headed toward the guy. The man turned and started walking toward the opposite staircase.

"Hey, I'm talking to you," Patrick called out.

The man picked up speed. Patrick sprinted forward. "Stop. Who are you?"

The man paused and turned with an exaggerated sigh. "Back off, sir."

Patrick halted a few steps from the guy, frowning. "Why are you following Miss Johnson?"

"Who?"

"You know very well who. I've seen you twice today. To often for it to be coincidence."

The guy shrugged. "Don't know what you're talking about."

"Did you smash up her car?"

"No."

"Make prank calls to her."

"No."

His impassive expression grated. "I don't believe you. I'm calling the police." Patrick pulled out his cell phone.

"That wouldn't be a good idea, sir."

Again with the *sir*. "Why not?"

"You don't want to get mixed up in this, Professor McClain."

How did the guy know who he was? Patrick straightened to his full six feet. "Are you threatening me?"

"Just giving some friendly advice." The man turned to step down the first stair.

Patrick pushed him up against the wall. "Don't walk away from me. I want to know who you are."

The guy pushed back, sending Patrick stumbling. He regained his balance and came at the guy again, taking him once again to the wall and putting his forearm at the guy's throat.

He pressed. "Who are you?"

Suddenly another man came vaulting up the stairs and body-slammed Patrick in the side. Pain exploded in his ribs and the air swooshed out of his lungs but he refused to loosen his grip.

Instead he sent the second guy sprawling on the floor with a kick.

Down the hall a door banged open.

Anne made a strangled sound and rushed forward. "Whoa, guys!" She laid a hand on Patrick's arm. "Stop, Patrick."

Confused by her words, Patrick turned his gaze on her. "Anne, get out of here. Call the police."

"Tell your boyfriend to back off now," the guy getting up from the floor said.

Not sure he could hold both men off and still protect Anne, Patrick let the first guy go and swiftly moved to stand in front of Anne. His heart slammed against his chest as he readied himself to defend her.

"Please let me handle this," Anne said close to his ear.

Shocked by her reaction but not willing to take his eyes off of the two men, Patrick asked, "Anne, what's going on?"

The second guy, the older one of the pair, said, "Miss Johnson, a word."

"She's not going anywhere with you," Patrick growled, his confusion mounting.

Anne took his fisted hand. "I never meant for you to get involved in this."

"In what?"

"Miss Johnson." The second guy's tone rang with warning.

She held up her free hand. "I know. I know."

Patrick turned the full force of his attention on Anne. Her eyes were wide, and a gamut of perplexing emotions crossed her pretty face. Doubt, anxiety, guilt.

A loop of unease wove through his chest, making his already bruised ribs ache. "Anne?"

Her mouth scrunched up and her gaze darted between the other men and Patrick.

Squeezing his hand, she finally let out a groan. "They're U.S. Marshals."

The shock hit him in the solar plexus. "What!"

"Miss Johnson!" the two men exclaimed simultaneously.

She positioned herself with her back to the men. Her eyes pleaded with Patrick to understand.

He didn't.

"I'm not who you think I am."

"Here we go…" the first guy muttered.

"Not here," the second guy ground out. "You cannot do this here."

Head spinning with bewilderment, Patrick tried to grasp the mean of the situation. "Marshals?"

"Yes, marshals." She lifted her head and stared him in the eyes. "I'm in the witness security program."

Staggered by that revelation, Patrick took a step back from Anne.

She released his hand, her eyes filling with tears. "You've been lying to me this whole time."

He was taking this badly.

Anne had hoped she could make it through the trial and not have to say anything to Patrick. She should have heeded Lidia's warning to not get attached to anyone.

But she had grown attached and now she had to deal with the consequences. If she was going to come clean with him, she might as well go the whole way.

She relaxed her throat and allowed her natural voice to come through. "Yes, I've been lying to you. Kind of."

He scoffed. "Kind of?"

"It was necessary." She turned to the two agents who'd introduced themselves to her as soon as she arrived this morning. The younger agent had said his name was Ford, like the car, and the older agent was Morris. "Tell him."

"It was necessary," Agent Ford stated dryly.

She made a face. "Thanks, that helps."

Agent Morris stepped closer. "Can we please take this out of the hall?"

Anne led the way to the office she'd been working in. She faced Patrick. "The only thing I haven't been truthful about is my name. My name is really Anne Jones."

He crossed his arms over his chest and peered at her through the lens of his glasses. "That accent is not from Los Angeles."

Heat burned in her cheeks. "Now I never said I was from Los Angeles. I said L.A. Which also stands for Lower Alabama."

He gave her a pointed looked full of sarcasm. "Right." He took off his glasses and wiped them with a cloth from his breast pocket. "I'm trying to wrap my brain around this. Your name is really Anne Jones and you're in the witness security program because…"

Remembering what his brother had gone through, she knew he'd understand. "Because I witnessed a murder."

He stilled, his long tapered fingers curling around his glasses. "Whose?"

Hoping he didn't bust the lens out of the frames, she said. "My boss. And several other men."

Patrick seemed to digest the information as he addressed the agents. "Is the murderer behind bars?"

Agent Morris answered, "For now. He's being held without bail through his trial. Anne is a key witness for the prosecution."

Patrick put on his glasses. "You're going to testify at the trial?"

"Yes. The agents say in less than three weeks." She held his gaze, losing herself in the chocolate depths.

"You're willing to risk your life to do this?"

The intensity in his question made her feel as if her answer was very important. "It's the right thing to do. I need to see justice done for my boss."

He nodded, his eyes taking on a determined gleam. "Where did it happen?"

"New Jersey. I worked at the Palisades Resort as a cocktail waitress while trying to get my big break on Broadway."

He arched an eyebrow. "You're a cocktail waitress?"

"No. I mean I worked as one to pay the bills, but I'm an actress."

"Indeed. And very good."

"Please don't take this all personally. I never meant to hurt you." This was what she was afraid was going to happen if she let him close.

His voice softened. "You could have told me."

"That's just it. I couldn't."

"And still shouldn't," Agent Ford interjected.

"I'm going to be straight with him," she stated, wishing the two agents would give them some privacy.

"And get both of you killed?" Morris said, his brown eyes challenging.

She frowned as doubt attacked her. "You said yourself that I was being paranoid. That the car, the rat and the calls weren't related."

"Rat?" Patrick touched her shoulder.

She grimaced at the memory. "I found a dead rat outside my apartment door."

Patrick moved closer to Anne, a protective gesture that wasn't lost on her. She'd never had a man be her champion before. He made her feel special, a feeling she decided she really liked.

"They all were related, weren't they?" Patrick demanded to know.

The two agents exchanged a glance. "We don't know. Domingo has a huge network," Morris stated.

"Then why did you tell me earlier I was safe and to go about my day?" Anne demanded.

Again the exchange of nonverbal communication between the agents. "There is no reason to believe your whereabouts have been compromised. We've been assigned to watch over you. If anyone does come after you, we'll intervene."

"You're using her as bait." Patrick nearly shouted.

"Of course not," Morris said, but there was a note of insincerity in his tone that raised the hairs on Anne's arm.

"But I'm going to suggest we relocate you," said Agent Ford.

Her stomach churned with anxiety and frustration. "I don't want to leave."

"If you change details. Add more men. It's only three weeks," Patrick countered.

"A lot can happen in three weeks," Morris said.

"And nothing might happen," Patrick replied.

The agents again exchanged glances. Morris moved toward the door. "I'm going to have to call this in. I'll tell them you want to stay but I won't recommend it."

"You don't have much choice if I leave the program," Anne stated, hating to play this game. This was her life they were talking about. "Agent Ford, would you mind leaving us for a moment?"

The agent nodded and left on the heels of his partner.

As soon as the door shut behind the agents Patrick settled his gaze on Anne. "You can't go back to your apartment."

Logically she knew he was right. Her stomach knotted with frustration. She liked her new life. She was beginning to know a few people at church and really enjoyed the town of Newton.

Unfortunately the agents were right, too. If she stayed out in the open now, she could put other people in danger. She sighed. "I suppose I should let WITSEC take me to a safe house."

"Or you could come home with me."

She blinked at the unexpected offer. "Your place?"

He shook his head. "Not my apartment. My mother's home."

She stepped back in stunned surprise. "No. I couldn't put her at risk."

He advanced a step and took her hands. "Listen to me. You'll be safe at my mother's. I'll make sure of it."

"How?" The man was a professor, not a bodyguard.

"My family has strong ties to the police department in Boston. I just have to say the word and we'll have protection."

"But would that be enough?"

"I'd stake my life on the Boston PD. Trust me."

His warm cocoa gaze drew her in, testing her heart, teasing her senses. She did trust him. Trusted that he believed he could protect her, that the friends of his family in the police department could provide her protection.

But if an assassin were really determined to kill her, could even the most dedicated and brave police officer be able to save her?

"I can't ask this of you," she whispered.

"You're not," he stated firmly, his expression determined.

Swallowing the doubts and fears, she nodded and placed her hand within his. She could only pray it wouldn't be the death of her. Or him. Or his family.

"Of all the underhanded, reprehensible things to do!" Lidia's fist pounded on the desk, the pain of the impact barely registering. She took a deep breath, but her constricted lungs wouldn't allow in more than a fraction of the air she needed.

"Take a seat, Lieutenant," said Special Agent in Charge Joseph Lofland.

He sat behind his wide oak desk, his tie perfectly knotted, his light brown hair neatly trimmed. Only his gray eyes conveyed the anger that Lidia felt. "Morris and Ford were following orders."

"Who ordered them to announce their presence?" she fumed.

"We want Domingo as much, if not more, than you," replied Lofland. "Showing her detail was a strategic move. She was never in danger."

"The girl reached out like she was told and your people let her leave the security of the WITSEC program."

"Any witness in the program is free to leave at any time. Anne Jones chose to reveal her identity."

"After your boys bungled their job," Lidia retorted and flopped down in to the leather chair opposite the desk.

Beside her Porter put a calming hand on her arm. He always had that effect on her. "Now we have to figure out how to keep Anne safe while not in the program and bring down Domingo."

She nodded, acknowledging his words. The only reason Lidia wasn't expounding on her anger was she knew that Anne was safe. One of her own NJPD people was watching her. And now according to the report that had just come in so was all of the Boston Police Department.

"And what about Maria Gonzales?" Lidia asked, thinking of the maid who'd also come forward with her account of seeing Domingo and his thugs enter the suite. Maria had been in the private bedroom at the time and had heard the voices in the hall.

She'd chanced a peek out just to have something to gossip with the other housekeeping staff. She'd already noted the other high stakes players that had entered the suite so when Domingo and his men had arrived she'd been disappointed. No call girls or anything that would suggest more than just a game of cards.

Except, not too much later, as Maria had finished changing the sheets on the bed, she'd heard the sound of gunfire. Terrified, she'd hid in the closet and had escaped after the massacre. But she'd recognized Domingo and seen him limping out of the suite, blood dripping down his pant leg.

She left the hotel and hidden out at her sister's in Queens and luckily Rick had found the woman before Domingo got wind of her.

"Please tell me you are watching her back."

Lofland seared her with a quelling look. "She is in good hands. Unlike Miss Jones, Maria is content to spend her days in a safe house."

Lidia's mouth twisted as his undertone of censure hit her. Neither she nor the FBI had been able to convince Anne to sit tight in protective custody until after the trial.

No, Anne had an independent streak that reminded Lidia of herself at that age. Twenty-five years ago. A lifetime ago. Now, nearing fifty, Lidia was ready to retire rather than exert her independence anymore than she had too. That was the beauty of youth. A person had the energy and conviction to stand their ground, just like Anne had insisted she wasn't going to sit twiddling her thumbs and wait. So she'd entered the program and taken the job at the college, changed her appearance and settled in. Only Anne had let herself get involved with Associate Professor McClain.

Lidia should have seen that coming. The two were exact opposites. And didn't opposites attract? Just look at her and Porter.

Lidia refused to think about the budding relationship with the D.A. when she needed to focus on the case.

She sat forward. "Look, is there anything either of you can do to speed up the court proceeding? The quicker we get Anne to testify the better."

Porter shifted, drawing Lidia's attention. His gaze held hers. "I'm pushing as hard as I can. But you can imagine Domingo's lawyer is pushing just as hard to delay the trial as much as possible."

Lidia snorted. "Yeah, so he can have time to get rid of the witnesses. All the more reason the judge should move things along."

"In light of the most recent events, I'm sure that the attorney general will step in and advocate with the court," Lofland stated.

"Let's call Dirkman and get on the fast track," Lidia demanded.

EIGHT

"Are you sure my coming here is okay?" Apprehension weaved through Anne's veins. She hoped she wasn't making a mistake.

"Yes, I'm sure," Patrick replied, taking Anne's hand and squeezing it in reassurance as he led her up the front steps of his childhood home. "I've already spoken to my mother and she is looking forward to meeting you."

"What about Princess?"

"Don't worry."

Anne wrinkled her nose and hugged the feline closer. *Easy for him to say.*

He opened the big wooden front door and ushered Anne inside. The scent of vanilla and sugar filled the air.

The bright cheerfulness of the home hit her full force, making her ache for such a life as this home represented. Family, love and respect. A place to be safe and comfortable. A life she could only dream about.

A gleaming hardwood floor stretched beneath her feet and extended into the living room to the left and the formal dining area to the right. A staircase with a polished mahogany banister led to the second floor. She could see the tiled floors and granite counters of the kitchen straight ahead.

The living room was a profusion of color against dark fabrics and wood paneled walls. Throw rugs and pillows of assorted shapes looked artlessly placed, yet the whole effect was very welcoming. All sorts of fresh flowers in vases of various styles filled every available space.

Anne's gaze landed on the gilt-framed oil painting above a beautiful mantel and fireplace. The McClain family stared back at her.

A handsome, uniformed man with dark hair and intense ebony eyes stood in the background. This picture was similar to the one in Patrick's apartment.

Flanking Mr. McClain on either side were two similarly dark-haired sons. Patrick stood a foot taller than the other boy, whom she assumed was Brody. Behind the ever present glasses, Patrick's eyes showed an amused sparkle that she had yet to see.

Though the young Patrick didn't have a smile on his face, he did lack that somber, stoic expression she'd grown accustomed to on the adult man.

Mrs. McClain sat in front of her husband, her long, ebony hair cascading over one shoulder and her crystal-blue eyes sparkling. A young girl stood beside her mother, their resemblance uncanny. Both possessed high cheekbones and fair skin. Megan McClain had also inherited her mother's blue eyes.

A small boy sat on Mrs. McClain's lap. Must be Ryan. His childish grin and the impish light in his dark eyes were captivating. She could only imagine how much more devastating this younger McClain must be as an adult male.

Such a lovely family. Sadness touched Anne's heart. This family had lost their father and husband not too many years after this portrait had been taken.

Such a senseless loss.

She didn't understand how God allowed such tragedy. But who was she to question Him? She didn't know His plans. His ways were beyond her comprehension. She could only hold on to her faith in a loving God and trust. Trust that He had a reason that couldn't be seen by the human eye.

Patrick tugged on her hand, urging her to follow him. His earnest, eager expression tripled her heartbeat.

Was he as nervous about her meeting his mother as she was? What if Mrs. McClain took a dislike to her? Could Anne take the rejection? Would his mother not want a cat in the house? What would Patrick do then? The questions ran through Anne's mind, tormenting her with insecurity and doubt.

They headed down the hall to the kitchen, with every step Anne's pulse picked up pace until the moment she crossed the threshold, where a woman with a long, dark braid was just taking out a tray of cookies from the oven.

Mrs. McClain's bright blue eyes lit on her son and then on Anne. She gave them a welcoming smile that twisted Anne up inside. Anne's own mother had never smiled with such warmth. Tentatively Anne smiled back and her blood slowed to a more normal rhythm.

Mrs. McClain sat the tray on the counter, wiped her hands on her apron and then moved to hug Patrick before turning her attention to Anne.

"I couldn't believe it when Patrick called. What a horrible thing for you to have to go through. But you're here now and we'll keep you safe."

"Mom, there's just one thing I forgot to mention."

Colleen raised her eyebrows. "Yes?"

Anne met his gaze. Mirth danced in his eyes.

"We'll have one other houseguest."

Anne suppressed a flutter of misgivings.

Patrick pointed to the animal in Anne's arms. "A cat named Princess."

Colleen smiled and reached out to pet Princess behind the ears. The cat snuffled into Mrs. McClain's hand and began to purr. "That's fine."

"I didn't think you'd mind," Patrick stated.

"Thank you." Though Anne wasn't so sure that she'd made the right decision. She couldn't stop the guilt flushing through her.

She shouldn't be here. This kind woman didn't deserve to have Anne's presence burdening her life.

"I don't think I should stay here. I appreciate your kindness but I should go." She turned to Patrick as anxiety clogged her throat. "I really should."

"We've already been through this. I thought you were going to trust me," he said, his voice soft. His eyes held a hint of hurt.

Anne wanted to, but doubts still lingered. What if something happened to these kind people because of her? She couldn't live with that.

"Is Princess an indoor or outdoor cat?" Mrs. McClain asked.

"Indoor," Anne replied tentatively. "You aren't allergic to cats are you?"

"No, dear." Mrs. McClain took Anne's hand and drew her to the kitchen nook. "Let's sit. Patrick, would you take Princess to Megan's room?"

Patrick held out his hands expectantly. Anne hesitated. Without Princess she felt even more vulnerable and alone. But Patrick was here and his mother was so nice. She held Princess up to eye level and said, "Be a good girl and go with Patrick." She handed her over and watched in amazement the way the feline curled against his chest.

He winked and walked out of the kitchen.

"Anne. May I call you Anne?"

She nodded, liking the compassionate and forthright way Mrs. McClain had about her.

"Would you like some iced tea?"

"That would be lovely. Thank you," Anne responded.

This was a woman of no nonsense. Anne could imagine she'd had to have been a strong woman to raise four kids by herself after their father died. Anne hoped some of that strength would rub off on her.

"I can understand your reluctance," Mrs. McClain stated in a calm and soothing tone as she sat a pitcher of tea on the table along with three tall glasses. "But please believe me when I tell you that you'll be safe here." She took a seat opposite of Anne. "The McClains have many friends within the Boston Police Department. Patrick's already arranged for around-the-clock surveillance while you're here."

Looking into this woman's kind and caring eyes Anne wished she'd had a mother as vibrant and committed. Her own mother had been tired and broken by life the last time Anne had seen her, over five years ago now.

Not for the first time Anne wondered how her family was doing. The minute she'd had her high school certificate she'd left the small Alabama town and never looked back. She'd been determined not to end up like her mama or her older sister, married to a jerk and with too many kids to feed.

Anne chose to believe Mrs. McClain, chose to put her safety in their hands. *Please, Lord, don't let me be making a mistake.* "I don't know what to say, other than thank you, Mrs. McClain."

"Please, call me Colleen."

Patrick joined them at the table.

"Aren't you heading back to the school?" Anne inquired as he made himself comfortable on the bench seat beside her. His big, warm body pressed along her side, providing her support and strength.

"I'm taking a vacation day."

His mom nearly choked on her tea. "That's a first."

Anne couldn't help but feel thrilled to know he was staying because of her. Too tired and frazzled to decipher or analyze his actions or her reactions, she would just go with it.

"So, Anne, tell me about yourself," Colleen said, her curious blues studying her. "Patrick said you're from lower Alabama. I've never been to that part of the country."

Trapped between the physical wall of the kitchen nook and the impenetrable wall of Patrick, Anne tried not to squirm. What she'd told Patrick still held true. She didn't want to talk about the past.

So instead she would focus on the last part of Colleen's statement. "Alabama's pretty in its own way. Lots of character. The town I grew up in had about one hundred people. We could go for miles without coming across another living soul. The Conecuh National Forest was our playground. Hide-and-seek among the plain pines and we'd skip rocks on the ponds. We'd pretend our old coon dog was captured by the Yankees and we had to rescue him."

"Weren't you afraid of the wildlife?" Colleen sat forward. "Aren't there alligators and snakes in the swamps in the South?"

Anne shrugged. "You leave 'em alone, they pretty much leave you alone."

"So your brothers...or sisters played in the forest with you?" Patrick asked.

Anne pressed her lips together. She didn't want to

discuss her family but she'd stirred the pot with her remark about playing in the forest. She slanted him a glance. "Two of each. During the hot days of summer we would float down the lazy Conecuh River on inner tubes."

She laughed softly, remembering. "My older brother, Tommy, once fell off his tube. He couldn't swim. None of us could. I still remember him floundering around until Josie, the eldest, shouted to him to stand up. That part of the river was barely knee deep.

"And then once, my younger sister, Mimi…I think she was four at the time, found a baby skunk out in the woodshed. She thought it was a cat. Mama 'bout had a fit. But Mimi was not going to let that baby go. Until it sprayed her after she pulled its tail. She smelled for a good month."

Colleen looked puzzled. "You have an accent. I hadn't noticed it before."

Anne winced. She hadn't realized she'd slipped into her natural voice.

"When was the last time you went home?" Patrick asked.

"A long time."

"It sounds like you miss your family," Colleen commented.

Deep in some part of Anne that she tried not to look at, she did miss them. But she couldn't go back. She'd burned that bridge when she took off. She could still hear her daddy's raging voice as she ran down the road toward the highway saying if she left, she'd better stay gone. A year after she'd run off, she'd written a letter asking if she could come back. Her letter had been returned unopened.

And she'd known she'd never be welcome back.

"I miss the outdoors. And I miss the simplicity of life," Anne admitted.

Colleen nodded in understanding. "Sometimes I think it would be easier to live in the days when there weren't so many cars and so many things distracting us from enjoying each day."

"Exactly. My family didn't have much. Almost no one did in the South. We worried about our needs not our wants, if that makes sense."

"It does," Colleen agreed. "Today people are so caught up in having the latest and greatest. I'm not saying there isn't value in all the technological advances but whatever happened to sitting down and writing a letter? No one writes letters anymore. If you want to communicate, you have to have a computer or a BlackBerry."

Patrick groaned. "Mom."

"What?" She stared at him. "You agree, right?"

He sighed. "I did until I met Anne."

Colleen raised her eyebrows. "Really? Do tell."

"She showed me how change can be worthwhile. That taking a chance on something new, something different, could be a good thing."

The glow of attraction Anne saw in his eyes entranced her, drew her in, making her lean slightly toward him. "Sometimes risk is necessary."

His gaze dropped to her mouth. "Yes, it is."

"It takes courage to change. To be open," Anne said.

"This is true," Patrick agreed.

He was so close, she could see herself in his eyes. "Like going to church?" The words popped out before she could stop them.

His eyes darkened and shuttered, closing her out. He leaned away. "I suppose."

"Church?" Colleen asked.

Anne's cheeks burned as Colleen eyed her with intense interest. "Patrick was kind enough to drive me to my church yesterday."

A pleased gleam entered Colleen's blue eyes and a smile touched her lips. "That's wonderful." She turned her piercing gaze to her son. "Maybe she can convince you to give God another chance?"

Patrick flinched. A tense silence filled the room. Anne didn't understand the dynamics going on but there was no mistaking the deep anguish etched in the lines of Patrick's face.

More than anything Anne wanted to soothe his hurt, but even with God's help, she didn't know how.

Later that evening after sharing a meal with Patrick and his mother, Anne stepped out into the sanctuary of the backyard. A brick patio extended about five feet, then a lush lawn, broken only by wood-rimmed flower beds and four distinctive trees that ended at a dark-stained fence encircling the yard. Over the patio, an arbor had been constructed and wisteria curled around the wooden slats.

According to Patrick, gardening was Colleen's passion. The immaculate landscaping gave credence to his words.

"You okay?" Patrick joined her beneath the arbor. His dark hair captured the illumination from the garden lamps. He'd removed his jacket and rolled up the sleeves of his button-down shirt. He'd also lost his tie and the top two buttons at his throat were undone revealing the rim of the undershirt beneath.

She drank in the sight of him in the evening twilight. "Yes. Being here is better than I expected."

His mouth quirked. "It's only been one day."

Bending to sniff a perfectly formed rose, she answered, "True." She straightened. He was so close, his masculine scent wrapped around her senses. More heady than the flower's perfume. "Are you staying here or going to your place?"

He leaned against the supporting beam of the arbor. "Would you like me to stay?"

She did, but she couldn't find the courage to say so. Trying to act nonchalant, she said, "It's up to you."

"Then I'll stay."

A warm radiance flowed through her. She tried to cover the reaction by changing the subject. "I really like your mother."

Colleen had a force of character that could only come from within, which could only come from a foundation of faith. After that uncomfortable moment when Colleen's remark had stirred the soul-searing pain that Anne had witnessed at the church, they'd managed to move the conversation forward to other topics, mostly due to Colleen's forthright personality.

"She likes you, too" he replied.

Questions burned on her tongue. Would he close her out again if she asked about his relationship with God? But she couldn't ignore what she'd seen or the way she'd ached inside for him. She'd come to care too much for him. "So what do you think about giving God a second chance?"

NINE

"I don't think about it."

This was way worse than she thought. His heart had hardened. Was there a chance she could soften him toward God, open Patrick to possibly reconciling with Him? "Did you grow up going to church?"

He crossed his arms over his chest "Did you?"

She pulled her gaze to his. Countering her question with one of his own was an avoidance tactic. She didn't want to tell him about her childhood, but she guessed he wouldn't open up unless she did.

Trust had to be earned.

There had been some ugliness in her past that made her cringe when she thought about it. Her parents hadn't lived by the faith they professed, which she supposed could have turned her completely against God, but hadn't. She could separate their actions from God. She knew enough about free will and human nature to know that what one professed with their mouth was not necessarily what was in their heart. She wanted her faith to be in her heart not just her words.

"I did grow up going to church. Every Sunday. In fact, the whole town went. Part of the culture of the South. All hundred of us would gather in the brick building and sing and listen to Reverend Tulane give his very impassioned sermons." She closed her eyes as memories flashed through her mind. "I can still see him standing at the altar in his black suit, waving the Bible as he talked about forgiveness, repentance and the love of the Lord."

She opened her eyes and gave a small laugh. "As a child I loved the stories in the Bible, but that's all they were to me. Stories. Because how could what the reverend said about God changing lives be true if on Monday Mama and Daddy weren't any different than they were on Saturday?"

"What were your parents like?"

Oh, she didn't want to go there. Shame heated her skin, making her overly warm. Their worlds were so far apart. Could he understand the kind of poverty she experienced?

Taking a seat on a wooden bench, she tried her best to forge ahead. "Daddy worked at the cotton mill. Mama stayed home with us kids, not because she wanted to, mind you, but there were very few jobs in our little corner of the world and the men got them. That's just the way things worked."

Patrick sat next her. "You said you have four siblings?"

"Yes." She took a deep fortifying breath before continuing. "We lived in a run-down trailer outside town. Town, being a relative phrase. A Piggly Wiggly and a Gas-N-Go were about the extent of it."

"And you left when?"

If he found her description of her childhood home distasteful, he had the good manners to keep it to himself. She laced her fingers and rubbed the palms together. "Just before my eighteenth birthday."

"What college did you attend?"

It was a legitimate question coming from a professor to his computer tech. It was a shame-inducing question coming from Patrick, the professor, to Anne, the hick from the sticks. But the Anne that had witnessed a murder and was being given a new chance to be someone else wanted to make up some fantastic tale that would awe and impress.

She could say she'd danced at Radio City Music Hall, sang at Carnegie Hall and performed in a play alongside some Tony award-winning actor. She could say she'd made her mark on Broadway instead of going to college.

She'd glimpsed deeper inside of him through his book than he presented to the rest of the world. And what she'd seen made her decide he deserved the truth—even if the truth offended his sensibilities.

"I never went to college. I have my high school certificate, that's it."

He studied her for a moment. "Then how do you know so much about computers?"

"Books. And I dated a techno geek when I lived in Manhattan."

"Amazing." There was no mockery in his tone. "That's right, you'd said you wanted to be an actress. So you headed to the Big Apple like a lot of other people."

"I did." He might as well hear it all. "I arrived in New York with just the clothes on my back and not a cent to my name."

"Why like that?"

She stared at the stars twinkling in the night sky, remembering how as a child she would wish upon the brightest light. "Because I ran away."

"From what?"

She blinked and dropped her gaze. "A bad relationship. The nearest high school was thirty miles away and big enough to have a decent football team. I started dating the quarterback. Everyone, my parents included, were sure Johnny had a good future ahead of him and thought I was lucky he'd picked me. My parents liked him."

She drew in a breath and gathered herself. "Johnny abused me. When I couldn't take the beatings anymore and broke it off, my daddy was livid. He thought I'd ruined my one chance to have a better life. We fought."

She made a face. "I said some things to him and my mama that were mean but true. Daddy backhanded me, like I'd seen him do to my mama, and I left. I did not want to end up like them."

He slid his arm around her shoulders, the gesture unexpected but oh, so nice.

"That's rough. And you haven't ended up like them. You made a conscious choice to live differently. That's admirable."

The warmth and concern in his voice comforted and thrilled. He wasn't disgusted by her Southern back roads beginning. "Yes." She had made different choices, though not always smart ones. "But not as rough as you losing your father."

He ignored her statement. "So how did you end up at the casino?"

She'd let his avoidance slide for now. "Acting's tough. New York's even tougher. I met a girl who got me connected in Atlantic City. The job paid well and Jean Luc was a good employer."

His arm tightened slightly. "And you saw him die."

She leaned her head on his shoulder as memories assaulted her mind. She shuddered. "It was horrible. So much worse than the movies ever make it seem. I thought I would die, too."

"I'm glad you didn't," he said.

His tender voice, almost a murmur, sent a pleasant shiver down her spine. "God spared me."

He jerked slightly at her words. "How did you get out alive?"

"I prayed and then Jean Luc fell literally to the ground beside me. Before he died he told me of a secret panel in the wall and gave me some cash to run with."

Patrick drew back to look into her face. "You didn't run?"

She lifted her head. "I couldn't. God gave me my life. I had to do what was right. I had to tell the police how Jean Luc and the others died."

"God didn't give you a chance, Jean Luc did."

"Only after I prayed. I know that sounds lame and far-fetched and even naive. But I know in my heart He's real and with me always. I can't pretend to understand Him or why there's so much bad in the world. I can only trust."

"You're noble and courageous, Anne Jones."

The awe in his voice and the gentle way his eyes caressed her face entranced and enflamed her. Affection unfurled and her heart jangled with a breathless anticipation. He was so much more than he appeared, so full of compassion and honor. A man who stirred her interest and made her feel special.

A giddy sense of excitement fluttered through her when she realized his attention wasn't brought on by her looks or what he thought he could get from her, but rather because he saw the person inside.

A delightful shiver ran up her spine. She shifted closer and turned more fully toward him. Attraction flared in his dark eyes, but he made no move to answer her silent plea. She pressed closer, tipping her head back, offering him her mouth, hoping he'd take advantage of the moment.

He touched her face, his hand gentle. He traced her cheekbone. Ran a finger lightly over her lips. Her blood quickened.

"It's getting late. We should go in."

His softly said words confused her until she realized he was slowly easing her out of his arms. She blinked back disbelief. Embarrassment flamed in her cheeks.

He stood and held out his hand. She slipped her palm over his. His strong fingers wrapped around her securely and led her into the house. She wanted to ask him why he hadn't kissed her, but she couldn't form the words.

He led her upstairs to the door of his sister's room where she'd be sleeping.

Even with the soft light of the hall, his expression was unreadable. "There are federal agents and police officers surrounding the property. I hope you will try to sleep well."

She nodded, unsure what to say or how to feel. He released her and walked further down the hall to disappear inside another room.

In a haze of confusion, Anne went into the bedroom.

A cat's meow distracted her. Princess sat regally on the foot of the bed, her white coat blending into the white fluffy comforter. The cat released another meow.

Taking the feline into her arms, Anne nuzzled her face into the soft fur. "Well, at least you love me."

The cat squirmed to be released.

"Or not." Anne loosened her hold and Princess jumped back on to the bed to settle on the pillow.

Anne tried to ignore the hurt in her heart as she readied herself for bed. But as she crawled beneath the covers, she couldn't help from chastising herself for not heeding Lidia's warning. *Don't get attached.*

Unfortunately for Anne, she was attached. Too bad Patrick wasn't.

* * *

Patrick sat in his old bedroom, staring out the window that overlooked the park across the street. Below on the road he could see the federal agent's unmarked car and in the opposite direction the Boston Police cruiser. And there were another set of each at the back of the house in the alleyway. There was no reason he shouldn't be snoozing away.

No reason other than the woman sleeping just down the hall.

His heart squeezed tight as the image of her upturned face and inviting eyes tortured him. He'd had to use every ounce of self-possession not to give in to kissing her. But she was vulnerable right now. She was hiding from people who wanted to kill her. The last thing she needed was for him to take advantage of her in such a susceptible state.

Admiration for her bravery and integrity filled his heart. From her humble beginnings to a witness for the prosecution.

Pretty amazing.

Her faith in God seemed so misguided, though. Co-incidence had saved her life. Yet…there was something so compelling about the way she trusted with her whole heart and soul.

Not Patrick.

His trust had been broken long ago, and there was no way God could ever earn that trust back.

* * *

The next day Anne helped Colleen in her garden, planting perennials and annuals Anne had never heard of before.

"You and Patrick seem to be getting along very well."

Anne sucked in a breath at the unexpected comment and inhaled a cloud of dirt from the spade she'd jerked upward at the same time. She coughed, then sputtered, "Uh, well. Yes."

Colleen sat back on her haunches and pushed at stray strands of hair that had come loose from her silver clip that secured the long, dark hair at her nape. Her jeans were faded and her red blouse streaked with dirt. "He's a good man. He's taken on so much responsibility over the years that he hasn't taken time to really live his life."

Anne's pulse beat double. "Because of his father's death," she ventured.

"He told you. That's good. He usually doesn't like to talk about it."

Anne thought about the remote and detached way he'd related the story to her. He hid his feelings behind that stony demeanor, but she now knew better. His book contained all the emotions he refused to show.

"He became the man of the house when he was still a kid. He just goes from one responsibility to another."

Anne closed her eyes as guilt chomped through her, leaving teeth marks across her soul. "Like me."

"Yes, frankly."

Wretchedness burned in her chest. No wonder he'd rejected her last night. She was just another burden to him. "I'm sorry."

Empathy and compassion blazed in Colleen's gaze. "We all do what's needed of us. He's helping you because then he feels needed."

There was no stopping the throb of despair welling inside. Was Colleen warning Anne not to get emotionally involved? It was too late for that. "I understand."

"Do you? I wonder."

Anne cocked her head. "What does that mean?"

The calculating gleam in the older woman's eyes confused Anne. "He may be telling himself he's doing this to help you, but I recognize the way he watches you."

She swallowed, almost afraid to guess what she meant. "Watches me?"

Colleen's mouth curved into a knowing smile. "I know my son. His feelings run deep, but he's so used to keeping his emotions under control that I've often worried he'd never allow love into his life."

"Love?" Anne squeaked.

"I may be jumping to conclusions."

Taking a deep breath to ease the tightness in her chest, Anne slowly exhaled before answering. "Yes, I think you are."

"I raised my boys to respect women and to not toy with their affections," Colleen said, her motherly voice coming through strong.

Anne's gaze jerked up. "Patrick isn't toying with my affections."

Colleen narrowed her gaze. "But are you toying with his?"

Aghast at the suggestion, Anne vigorously shook her head. "Of course not. Patrick's a great guy. I wouldn't hurt him for the world."

Colleen seem to be satisfied. "Good. I'm glad to hear that."

Anne wasn't sure what to make of the exchange. Was Colleen warning her off or trying to play matchmaker?

Colleen stood and dusted the dirt from her knees. "I've always believed that when Patrick finally gave his heart to a woman, she'd have to be a special woman."

Well, that ruled her out. Anne dropped her gaze to the hole she'd dug wishing she could crawl inside.

A hand on her shoulder lifted her gaze.

"You're a very special woman, Anne Jones."

Colleen winked and then went inside, leaving Anne reeling from her words.

Definitely matchmaking.

Darkness blanketed the house, but the man knew there were other men standing guard. Two outside and two inside. He'd been monitoring their activity and now the time to act had come. As always dressed in black, he crawled military fashion across the dry grass toward the dining room window where an old, full rhododendron would provide him cover as he cut through the glass and entered the house.

Once in the dining room, he paused to listen. The soft sound of rubber soles on linoleum told him at least one guard was in the kitchen using only the moon's illumination as light. The man edged toward the arched entry that led to the living room and the stairs. This time he had both his sheathed knife and a gun with a silencer in a holster at his shoulder as his weapons.

He took the stairs two at a time, careful not to step near the middle where the wood might creak and give him away.

As he reached the landing, a inky shape, bulky and close, rammed into him, sending him off balance and down a few steps.

"Stop!" came a shouted command as the stairwell was flooded with light.

With a quick yank, the man drew his gun and fired two shots at the federal agent descending the stairs. Realizing that he'd miscalculated, the man abandoned his quest. The target would have to wait for another day. Being caught was not an option.

He ran down the stairs as the agent that had been in the kitchen skidded to a halt, his weapon drawn, but the man was ready and fired off a shot that hit the agent square in the forehead.

The man hit the light switch, throwing the house back into darkness just as the front door banged open. The man sprinted to the dining room and out the window. He heard the shouts of the remaining agents. Not taking the caution he'd used in approaching the house, the man ran headlong for the copse of trees at the edge of the property where his car waited.

Within minutes he disappeared down the highway.

"Dirkman wants the witnesses brought in for a run-through before they take the stand," Porter told Lidia as she entered his office and took a seat in the leather chair across from his desk.

They seemed to be doing this a lot lately. He'd call, she'd come to his office and then they'd head to dinner. She found herself looking forward to the evenings when she wasn't working. She hadn't done that in years.

Tonight they were on the job.

It was standard practice to prep witnesses before the trial, but Lidia couldn't help anxiety from twisting inside her gut. Somewhere in the system they had a leak. A leak they had yet to plug. A surge of anger rode a high tide through Lidia's blood.

One witness was dead. Nikki had been right. They hadn't been able to protect her. Guilt and frustration stabbed at Lidia's conscience. She should have tried harder to get the girl to agree to protection. Maybe she wouldn't be dead now.

Anne was no longer in the program but stashed in Boston, in a civilian's house no less, though thankfully safe for the moment. But for how long?

Unfortunately the safe house where the third

witness, Maria Gonzales, had been was ambushed last night. Maria made it out alive thanks to the surviving two out of the four original agents guarding her. She was now safely hidden in another secure location. One only she, Porter and Lofland knew about.

"Can't you go to the witnesses?" she asked, fearing that bringing them in before their scheduled time would only put them in more danger.

He nodded. "That's what I was thinking. I was hoping you'd come with me."

An unexpected flush of happiness cascaded over Lidia. She'd planned on demanding to accompany him, but this…this was so much better. He wanted her with him. They would make a good team. A work team.

She knew better than to think further than the immediate. Life took unforeseen turns that could leave a person floundering.

But she still couldn't help the burst of pleasure from making her smile. "I'd love to join you."

TEN

Lidia and Porter arrived in the wee hours of the morning at the two-story corner house with green trim across from a park. They were greeted by tall, dark and tweed. Patrick McClain she guessed correctly.

They showed their identification and were admitted.

The house, shrouded in darkness except for the hall light, exuded a kind of comforting warmth Lidia sorely lacked in her own life. The place she called home was a small ranch in the suburbs with about as much charm as a carport.

This was a good place for Anne to be, Lidia decided as she and Porter followed Patrick to the kitchen. Anne sat at the kitchen nook table with another woman. A lit candle on the table glowed brightly, the light bouncing off the flowered walls and outlining the two women with halos of illumination.

Anne jumped up and came to hug Lidia. Lidia tried not to let the emotion welling up take hold, but it was good to see the young woman looking so much better than she had when Anne had told her story of watching Jean Luc die.

Lidia held Anne at arm's length. "You changed your hair."

Anne touched the short layers of red. "The new me," she quipped.

The older woman stood, Anne introduced them. Mrs. McClain's frank, accessing gaze washed over Lidia.

"Mrs. McClain." Lidia held out her hand.

Accepting her hand, Mrs. McClain inclined her head. "Lieutenant."

Lidia introduced Porter. "This is District Attorney Christopher Porter."

Porter stepped forward to shake hands with Mrs. McClain and then her son. "Thank you for allowing us to come at such an odd hour."

"We understand," Mrs. McClain assured them. "I thought the kitchen table would serve you best."

Lidia and Porter exchanged glances. The layout of the house with the kitchen at the rear and then the yard beyond made a much safer place to conduct their interview. Less likelihood that a sniper on a roof could find a clean shot.

"Perfect," answered Porter.

Anne slid back into a seat. Porter took the seat opposite of her and laid his briefcase on the table.

Lidia turned to the two McClains. "Would you mind giving them some privacy?"

Mrs. McClain nodded. "I'll go back to bed. Patrick,

please lock up after our guests." She kissed her son's cheek before padding out of the room.

Lidia arched an eyebrow at Patrick. She could see by the stubborn jut to his jaw he didn't like having to leave Anne. Lidia could appreciate his protectiveness and obviously, despite her warning to Anne not to get attached, the two had developed feelings, but she had a job to do. "Professor?"

He inclined his head. "I'll be in the living room." To Anne he said, "Call me if you need me."

"I will," she said, her eyes wide and fixed on him.

When he left, Lidia came to the table. "Anne, why do you have purple eyes?"

Anne grinned. "You said to change my appearance."

"That I did." Shaking her head, Lidia sat down and gestured for Porter to begin.

Two hours later, Porter seemed satisfied. "You've done well, Miss Jones."

Lidia took Anne's hand. "The morning of the trial, a team of U.S. Marshals will escort you back to New Jersey."

She blinked. "You won't be with me?"

Lidia shook her head. "No. But I will be at the trial as the arresting officer."

"Miss Jones, don't be disturbed if during the court proceedings you grow emotional," Porter commented as he gathered his notes together and slipped them into his briefcase.

Anne bit her lip. Anxiety curled in her abdomen. "It will be hard to see Mr. Domingo again."

"You won't be alone," Lidia said, drawing Anne's gaze. "We'll be there. And I have a feeling the professor won't be letting you out of his sight."

Anne shook her head. "I'm sure he'll be glad when this is over so he can get on with his life."

Lidia's expression clearly stated she thought Anne didn't know what she was talking about. "Oh, come on. The minute I walked in here and saw the way that man looked at you, I knew. The man has it bad for you."

A quiet laugh of disbelief escaped even as her heart beat an erratic tattoo in her chest. "No. You're wrong. He doesn't…does he?"

Lidia slid a glance at Porter. They seemed to communicate without words. Curious. Anne suddenly had the distinct impression that there was something going on between the two. Good for Lidia. She deserved some happiness.

Anne squeezed Lidia's hand to gain her attention. Giving her a pointed look, she said, "I could say the same about you."

Lidia's eyes widened and red crept up her neck. "Okay. Enough." Lidia released her hand and stood. "We'll see you in a few days."

Anne followed them to the front door. Patrick came out of the living room where he'd apparently been reading. He shook hands with Porter and Lidia before they left.

The full impact of what she was doing hit Anne.

In a few days she'd be sitting on the witness stand

facing the man whom she saw kill Jean Luc Versailles. She shivered all the way to her toes.

"Cold?" Patrick asked as he slid his arm around her shoulders.

Not now. Anne raised her gaze to his. "Just nervous about the trial."

He nodded. "I don't blame you. But you're doing the right thing. And I'll be with you every step of the way."

Relief and gratitude swept through her. She needed him to be with her like she'd never needed anyone else in her life. Boy, was she glad to have his support.

She tried to read his expression, to see past his defenses into his thoughts, but she couldn't. Did he care for her even a little or was she really just a responsibility he'd taken on like any other?

Please, Lord, let this...this thing between us be more than mere responsibility or neediness.

Did she dare pray for love?

"You're going to have to control that temper of yours, Raoul," Evelyn Steiner remarked.

Raoul tolerated the female lawyer because she was sharp. Sharp eyes, sharp intellect and sharp tongued. Today, she'd pulled her graying-brown hair so tightly into a bun that even her features were sharp.

He'd always found having a woman lawyer both amusing and useful. People tended not to believe that a lady like Evelyn, with her thousand-dollar pumps and Chanel suits, would defend a man whom she thought anything but innocent.

Ha! Evelyn was one of the shrewdest and craftiest people Raoul knew. That's why he paid her the big bucks.

Now sitting across from her in a private room where there were no guards listening, Raoul relaxed his hunched shoulders. First thing he was gonna do when he got out, after he smeared that smug look off that lady cop's face, was have a massage.

There was this little blonde over in Newark who could make a man scream with those strong hands of hers. "Yeah, yeah. I know. Keep it cool in court. But it's never going to get that far."

Evelyn raised a perfectly shaped eyebrow. "You know something I don't?"

Raoul smirked. "Can't have a trial if there ain't no witnesses."

Narrowing her stone-cold eyes, she said, "Don't go mouthing off. The D.A. is aiming for the death penalty. You need to be focused."

She cleared her throat. "I've filed a motion for continuance but that's been denied. I've filed a motion to suppress two of the witnesses because they can only put you and your two boys in the room, but the judge is being stubborn. So much hangs on this one girl."

She pulled out a file. "Anne Jones from Alabama. I'll do what I can to discredit her, but there doesn't seem to be any skeletons to dig up. In fact, she's too perfect. From a dirt poor family. Left for New York after High School. Had a few boyfriends, but so far nothing to hold against her. By all accounts, she's a hard worker and a decent person."

The image of the blonde running toward the mirrored wall, her blue gaze colliding with his in the reflection, flashed in Raoul's mind. Rage tightened his throat, once again tensing his shoulders.

She wasn't supposed to have been there. He'd been told only of the two card players that would make up the foursome.

Had Raoul known about the waitress he'd have taken her out first. Women had a way of messing everything up.

Raoul leaned forward, piercing Evelyn to her seat. "You let me worry about the girl. You just do your legal magic, like a nice little puppet."

Evelyn's lip curled. "Careful, Raoul. That client/ lawyer privilege only goes so far."

Molten fury clouded his vision for a moment. "Are you threatening me?"

Her lips thinned into a semblance of a smile. "Making sure you know that respect goes both ways." She waited a heartbeat before continuing. "Now, let's get you prepped. Just in case."

Raoul deliberately banked his roiling temper. When this was over, there would be several female skeletons for the grave diggers.

Anne paced the backyard of the McClain home. She was supposed to be planting more flowers in a bed near the garden gate, but she found staying in one spot difficult.

The late afternoon sun touched her where the

sleeveless top and shorts she'd borrowed from Megan's drawers exposed her skin. The heat of the patio bricks on her bare feet brought a measure of comfort, and the aroma of roses, wisteria and earth worked to calm her stretched nerves.

She was to testify tomorrow. Lidia and the D.A. were confident that with Anne's testimony Jean Luc's murderer would be brought to justice. Patrick promised to support her through the trial, but the question that kept running across her mind was what would happen after the trial?

Would she go back to New York and continue her pursuit of a career on Broadway? Did she even want that now?

If not that, then what? What would she do with herself? And would Patrick be in the picture? Or once he was no longer needed, would he gladly walk out of her life?

Her head began to pound with the confusing and upsetting thoughts.

She felt trapped in the backyard. The balmy spring air added to the sensation of oppression, like a huge hand of heat pressing down on her, making her sweat. She wanted to go for a walk, to be out in the open and not be afraid.

But she had to get through the next few days. She went back to the flower bed and tried to clear her mind as she put the plants into the ground.

Just as she was finishing with the last plant in the flat, Patrick came into the yard. He wore brown slacks and a striped button-down shirt with the sleeves rolled up. His work clothes. He stared at her, his gaze assessing and interested, before walking across the patio to the flower bed.

Growing uncomfortable under his intense study, she asked, "Did Sharon get your password accounts set up?"

He nodded, his head tilting one way and then another as he peered at her through the lens of his glasses. His eyebrows went up. "Your eyes. They're blue."

She grinned sheepishly. "I was wearing contacts before."

"Ah." He waved his hand to her hair. "Are you really a redhead?"

She shook her head, touching the sheared ends. "I was born a towhead actually."

"The purple was unique, but blue eyes suit you."

She couldn't help a little quaver of anticipation deep inside of her. "I hope that the real me will be okay."

"Of course," he replied. "My brother Ryan will be joining us for dinner tonight."

"Oh. That's unexpected." She wasn't sure how to feel about meeting one of Patrick's siblings and becoming that much more enmeshed in his family. Surely heartache only lay down that path.

"Yes, well. That's Ryan. He's heading out of town and called to say he'd be stopping by. Mother has informed our guards already."

"That's good, because we certainly wouldn't want Ryan to be mistaken for an assassin," she quipped.

Patrick's eyes darkened with concern and a frown appeared between his eyebrows. "No, we wouldn't."

Whew! The man needed to lighten up. She looped her arm through his. Her heart seemed to rush to the places all along her side where she touched him. Talk about overheating. "Ease up there, Professor. It's going to be a good night," she pronounced.

Because come tomorrow she had a serious job to do. And she needed him to be ready to catch her if she botched it.

"It was really nice meeting you, Ryan," Anne said as the youngest McClain was about to take his leave after a delicious dinner and extremely enjoyable evening. Anne's sides hurt so bad from laughing; she could hardly remember the last time she'd had such a good time.

Patrick and Ryan were more different than any two brothers could be. Where Patrick was calm and reserved in tweed, Ryan's hip designer clothes, and hyperenthusiasm and charm both entertained and overwhelmed.

And watching the way Colleen handled each son according to their temperament was a lesson in parenting that Anne had never witnessed before.

Colleen drew out Patrick and reined in Ryan simultaneously. It was truly fascinating.

Ryan gave Anne a crushing hug. "You be strong."

Colleen had asked Anne's permission to reveal her story, since her presence affected their family. Anne couldn't see a reason to keep it a secret.

Anne laughed and gently eased out of his arms. "I will. You have a safe trip. I'd much rather be heading off to Maui tomorrow than New Jersey."

Ryan's dark eyes gleamed. "Maybe one day Patrick can take you to the islands."

For a moment Anne went speechless and she could feel blood flooding her face. Did matchmaking run in the family, or what?

Jaw set in a tight line, Patrick put his hand on Ryan's shoulder and maneuvered him toward the door. "Have a safe trip, little brother. Let us know when you get back."

Colleen stepped between them. "Boys, mind your manners." She kissed Ryan's cheek. "Be careful and call when you land."

Ryan's smile softened. "I will, Mom. I'll bring you back something fun and pretty."

"Just come back," the McClain matriarch commanded.

Ryan waved and disappeared out the front door. Anne avoided checking Patrick's gaze as she made her way to the back patio. She still couldn't believe his brother's bold statement. It was one thing for her to hope that the future would include Patrick but another entirely for someone else to put that hope to voice.

The night sky twinkled with a million stars, making the heavens glitter. The air had a bite to it. Anne was glad she'd put on the sweater set along with the long skirt she had had brought over from her apartment. She planned on wearing the outfit tomorrow at the trial because it was feminine yet modest.

"I'm sorry for Ryan's big mouth," Patrick stated when he came out of the house and joined her in the backyard.

Waving away his concern, she said, "He's a kick. I enjoyed him."

"Indeed," Patrick replied, his gaze on something over her shoulder.

She turned to see what he found so interesting. The back gate was cracked opened. A cold shot of alarm trapped her breath somewhere between her lungs and her throat.

"Go back inside," Patrick ordered as he stalked toward the gate.

She reached out to stop him. "Don't!"

Too late. He went out the gate. The world slowed as she waited, standing there alone in the garden, fearing that Patrick wouldn't return. Knowing that if anything happened to him, it would destroy her.

In a moment of intense understanding she realized she loved him. Oh, man.

She sank to the ground. Each passing second that Patrick didn't return felt like a knife twisting in her abdomen.

There was a movement near the gate. She gasped. Then Patrick materialized out of the shadows and rushed to her side. Giddy relief brought tears to her eyes.

"What's wrong?" He gathered her in his arms. "Are you hurt?"

Shaking her head, she touched his face. "No. I just got scared. You left and I was alone and I was afraid you wouldn't come back and I thought he'd gotten you and—"

"Shh." He put a finger to her lips. "I'm here."

For a moment she soaked in his presence, allowed the comfort, the support, he offered to wrap around her like a protective shield, because she feared all too soon, once the trial was over and he resumed his life, he'd be only a memory and she'd once again be alone. Forcing herself to rein in her emotions, she asked, "Did you see anything?"

"Our guards are all where they should be. I told them about the unlatched gate. They'll keep a watch out."

"Good. I feel so silly for panicking."

He helped her to her feet. "You have reason for being on edge. But soon it will be over and you can start your life over again."

She so wanted to ask if he'd be a part of her new life, but the words stuck to the roof of her mouth. Now was not the time to see where their relationship was headed. She knew better than to make decisions in the midst of a crisis.

So much hinged on the next few days.

Her life and the love growing in her heart for Patrick.

ELEVEN

Carlos sat in the metal chair in the prison visitors' area across from his uncle, and was thankful for the Plexiglas that separated them. Carlos hadn't even told his uncle the bad news yet.

"Uh, well, one pigeon got away," he said. He cringed at the molten rage filling his uncle's face.

"What are you going to do about it?" Raoul ground out.

Carlos swallowed back the panic churning in his stomach. "That one can't be caught again. At least not yet. The handlers are being very hush-hush."

Raoul leaned forward, his palms flat on the metal shelf in front of him. Carlos could see the beads of sweat along his uncle's forehead. Carlos wished he had the guts to tell his uncle to take a flying leap but…Carlos couldn't. He had no doubt Uncle Raoul would make him pay if he dared. And when Raoul called in a debt, people suffered. Carlos didn't like pain and didn't want to suffer.

Carlos kind of hoped his uncle would stay behind bars, but for men like Raoul, laws didn't matter and prisons weren't enough to curtail power. So Carlos would do what he must to stay in his uncle's good graces, and thus stay alive unharmed.

"Don't worry, Uncle. We've got time before hunting season is over. We'll snag a big bird and dine for weeks," Carlos said, trying to sound self-assured and confident.

"You get that bird, nephew, fast. Or the last thing you'll need to worry about is food."

Carlos shuddered. "I will, Uncle. I will."

From the farthest corner of the garden, deep in the shadows the man watched as Patrick walked the woman into the house.

Frustration kicked him in the gut. He hadn't anticipated that the woman would come out into the yard at the exact moment that he'd slipped in. She'd been too far away to slit her throat without giving her a chance to sound an alarm.

He'd had a pitiful few seconds to decide to hide without relatching the gate.

He planned to kill the woman and get away without being caught. One miscalculation wasn't going to change that. He'd just have to adjust his plans.

He knew the schedule of the security teams outside. He'd been watching them for the past two nights. He had timed his approach to coincide with the police officer's change in shift and then crept along the darkened alley to wait another hour for the fed's shift change. He'd taken advantage of that precise moment to slip through the gate.

But then she'd walked out. Closely followed by the professor.

Too bad McClain had noticed the gate so quickly and put the men outside on the alert. Dumb luck, that.

Now the man would have to wait longer until they were settled in their cozy little beds before he could do away with the woman. One quick slit of his knife and she'd wouldn't be talking to anyone ever again.

Easy enough.

Now he just had to wait.

Patrick sat at the desk in the upstairs den, his home computer up and a new story staring at him, waiting for the words to flow across the screen. But he couldn't process his thoughts into any coherent idea. All he could think about was Anne.

At every turn the woman left him off-kilter and holding his breath to see what other surprises she had for him. And he really couldn't say he resented or re-gretted the roller-coaster ride she was taking him on.

His mother liked her, more than the few other women he'd brought home over the years.

And Ryan had gushed all over Anne like a love-struck puppy. But then again, that was Ryan. He charmed the women and then left them wanting more. Though Anne had seemed to enjoy Ryan's attention, Patrick had realized quickly that Anne hadn't taken Ryan very seriously.

Interesting.

Patrick had to admit he was relieved. The burst of possessiveness had caught him off guard when Ryan had hugged Anne. His brother's overly demonstrative way had always boggled Patrick's mind, but tonight it had downright irritated him.

Rubbing at his gritty eyes, he glanced at the clock. Only a few more hours before the marshals would arrive to escort Anne back to New Jersey. Patrick stretched and decided he'd better at least try to rest so his brain would be alert for tomorrow. He shut down his computer, and then headed to bed.

After the trial, he'd see where this relationship with Anne was headed. He wasn't sure in what direction he wanted the relationship to go but he did know he wanted her in his life. The only question was, would she want *him* in her life?

Anne couldn't sleep. She tossed and turned, disturbing Princess who hissed a warning of discontent every time Anne shifted. Finally Anne decided to give up on sleep for the night. She slipped out of bed and wrapped the warm robe Colleen had pulled out of Megan's closet around her and stuffed her feet into a pair of fuzzy slippers.

She shuffled to the window and stared out at the moon so high in the dark sky. Light spilled over the street below, outlining the Boston Police cruiser and the federal agents four-door sedan.

Anxiety burned in her stomach. They were on the home stretch now and she couldn't wait for this all to end.

A noise behind her raised the hair on her nape. The doorknob turned. Patrick?

The dark silhouette of a man, who clearly was not Patrick, entered and closed the door before stealthily moving toward the bed. She pressed into the darkened corner of the room. Her heart thudded in her chest.

Stifling the scream building inside of her, Anne edge along the hall toward the door. Her side collided with the dresser. She winced as the dark figure whipped around. A long knife glinted in the moonlight.

Anne let loose a scream.

Just as Patrick began to doze off a woman's scream split the air.

Jolted awake, he bolted from his bed and out the door. He didn't hesitate, running straight for his little sister's room. Anne's room.

He burst through the door and hit the light switch. His gaze landed on Anne, pinned against the dresser and struggling with a man dressed in black wielding a nasty looking knife in his tight fist.

He recognized the wiry, dark-haired man. He'd seen him standing on the street outside Anne's apartment the morning he'd picked her up for church. The assassin the FBI had feared.

Adrenaline and rage pumped through Patrick's veins and thundered into his ears. Undeterred by the weapon, Patrick lunged at the man, using his shoulder to push the man away from Anne. They landed with a thud on the floor.

The intruder rolled away and jumped to his feet, the knife swooshing through the air in an arc.

Patrick came to his feet, blocking the door and keeping himself between the assassin and Anne. "Go, Anne. Get the agents!"

The man jabbed his weapon at Patrick with practiced precision, trying to force him back.

"No!"

Anne's scream galvanized Patrick into action. He swiped the sweater that Anne had worn earlier from the back of the small vanity chair, and wrapped it around his left arm. Using the bulk on his forearm as a shield, Patrick moved in, closing the gap between him and the intruder.

The assassin thrust the knife forward, slicing through the protective sweater.

Patrick barely felt the sting of the knife. Calling on old lessons, he took advantage of the moment to use the knuckles of his other hand in a downward arc to rap forcibly across the forearm of the hand that held the knife, hitting the radial nerve and causing the man to drop the weapon with a pain-filled yelp.

Before the man could make another move, Patrick followed with a sharp jab of his foot to the side of the man's right knee, eliciting a scream as the leg buckled, bones snapping. The man dropped to the floor, withering in agony.

The pounding of footsteps echoed in Patrick's adrenaline-laced mind. Hands pulled him back as he continued to lunge forward, intent on causing the villain more harm.

Two police officers maneuvered him out of the way.

"Patrick, Patrick. Let them take care of this," Anne's urged, her gentle hands holding his arm.

"You're okay?" Patrick blinked as the rage receded. His breathing came in labor huffs. The room became a sea of uniformed officers and federal agents. He looked into Anne's clear blue eyes. The concern and tenderness there calmed his racing heart.

She nodded. "But you're bleeding."

Bright red blood seeped through the sweater she'd planned to wear the next day to court. "Minor compared to what could have happened."

Reality hitting her, Anne shuddered. He could have been killed defending her life. Her heart pitched and a mix of guilt and gratefulness spread over her. She didn't deserve such a wonderful knight in…black silk pajama bottoms and a red T-shirt.

An officer spoke into the mic at his shoulder. "We need a bus." He gave the dispatcher the address for the ambulance.

A federal agent stepped over to Patrick. "Good job. You broke his leg."

"Would have liked to have broken his neck," Patrick muttered.

The agent's lips thinned. "If you had we wouldn't be able to question him. At least this way, the man's at our mercy."

Patrick grunted. The agonized curses and moans of

the fallen man filled the air. Anne turned away, not wanting to feel compassion for the man's pain. He'd tried to kill her, but even that knowledge couldn't snuff out the empathy twisting in her heart.

"Anne? Patrick?" Colleen McClain stood in the doorway, her long hair unbound and her robe held tightly at the neck. Her worried gaze took in the scene in the room.

"We're both okay, Colleen," Anne answered.

"Patrick, you're bleeding," Colleen rushed forward.

"Just a scrape, Mom," Patrick assured her.

Colleen searched his face before turning her gaze to Anne. "You two should wait downstairs for the medics. I better go put on a pot of coffee since none of us will be sleeping much tonight."

Patrick stared after his mother. "That was odd."

Anne pulled him toward the stairs. "Something other than a man breaking into your house and trying to kill me?"

"Yes. My mother."

Anne led him into the living room and made him sit on the couch. "What was odd about your mother?"

"She didn't try to take over."

Anne sat beside him and averted her gaze from the bright red stain spreading through the sweater, instead she focused on his face. The color had leached from his skin. Was he going into shock?

She needed to keep him alert and talking until the paramedics arrived. "Is your mother usually the take-charge type?"

He shrugged. "The motherly type."

Didn't he realize how blessed he was to have a mother so willing to be a parent? "I don't understand what the problem is."

"She left me in your care."

Anne stilled. That hadn't been lost on her. His mother had clearly giving the reins of his care to her once she realized his injury wasn't life-threatening. "I guess she feels I'm capable of keeping you sitting while we wait."

"You were holding off that guy pretty well. You have some well-disguised muscles."

Muscles or not, Anne had never been so frightened in her whole life or had fought so hard. As terrifying as witnessing a brutal murder had been, being attacked had been worse. "I'm glad you came when you did. And as for muscles, climbing trees as a child and carrying trays filled with drinks may have built up some strength, but what you did took skill. You didn't learn those moves in dance class."

"Mom may have thought we all needed to be graceful, but dad thought we needed to know how to fight."

"So that was some kind of martial arts?"

"No. Good old-fashioned street fighting."

"Very effective," she said, impressed and a bit awed. Every day that passed Patrick allowed her glimpses of the amazing man he was beneath the professor persona. "Did your siblings learn as well?"

He inclined his head. "Yes. I made sure they all

were taught just as I had been. That's what my dad wanted."

"Is it because of your father's death that you've given up on God?" Surprised at herself for her boldness, she held her breath.

The soft light of the table lamp bathed his pale features in a warm glow but the shuttered expression in his eyes frosted the air. "God betrayed me. Betrayed all of us."

She silently sent up a prayer of guidance. She wasn't equipped to help him come to terms with God's ways. "I don't know why your father had to die, but I do know God didn't do it."

"He's in control right? Omnipotent, all powerful?"

Bitterness laced his words, but also a deep hurt that made her ache inside.

"But he gives us free will. Your father chose to respond to the call. He chose to get out of the car." She winced. She was mucking this up. She didn't want him to think that blame rested solely on his father. "The man who shot him made a choice. We all make choices. And every choice a person makes has a ripple effect and touches other people's lives."

"I've heard this before." He waved his uninjured hand, his expression dismissive. "It still doesn't explain why God didn't intervene. Why God chose to ignore my prayers of safety for my father."

His pain gutted her. Hadn't she had that same thought when she first entered the McClains's house? She wished she could make Patrick's hurt go away. "I don't have an answer to that. All we can do is choose to love and to trust."

He seemed to weigh her words, his eyes staring into hers as if searching for something. What else could she say? Her own faith was so tender and full of discovery, how could she possibly help him to accept God's love?

A commotion at the front door drew their attention. The EMTs arriving. Patrick stood as an officer directed a young African-American woman over to attend Patrick's wound.

Her name tag read, Keller. "Hello, sir. Let me take a look."

Knowing now was not the time to pursue their discussion, Anne watched as the EMT unwound the bloodied sweater from Patrick's arm. Anne's stomach pitched at the sight of the gash slicing across him forearm.

"This is shallow. You won't have any permanent damage," remarked Keller. She turned to wave at an officer standing by. "CSU is going to want a picture of this."

The office nodded and hurried away. When he came back, another man followed carrying a camera. He snapped off several shots of Patrick's arm, before Keller shooed him away. Keller then used butterfly bandages to close the wound. "Keep it dry until you can get in to see your regular doctor."

Loud yelling split the air as the would-be assassin, strapped to a gurney, was carried down the stairs by two other EMTs.

"I have rights!" the man screamed. "I want my lawyer!" As they passed through the hall toward the front door, the man spit at Anne and Patrick.

"Lovely," Anne stated dryly.

One of the FBI agents approached. "We've identified your assailant. His name's Rico Trinidad. We'll find his connection to Domingo. In the meantime, we need to move you to a more secure location."

Disappointment and dread slumped Anne's shoulders. She didn't want to leave, but she knew for the McClains's sake she should.

"Why?" asked Patrick. "You don't honestly think anything else will happen tonight do you?"

"We can't be sure. This location was compromised," explained the agent.

Patrick shook his head. "She's not going anywhere. You'll have to figure out a way to keep her safe here."

Anne couldn't believe Patrick still wanted her to stay even after the intruder. She wanted to question him, ask him why? Did his feelings run deeper than responsibility? But those questions would have to wait until the right time. Now was not that time.

After the trial, when their lives could go back to some semblance of normal. Then she'd ask and she'd tell him of her feelings.

The agent turned to Anne. "Miss Jones?"

"I'll stay," she said softly.

The agent nodded. "Then I will post agents inside as well as outside."

"Fine," agreed Patrick and then put his arm around

Anne and directed her toward the stairs. "We have a few hours."

Anne scoffed. "Yeah, like I'm going to sleep now."

He touched her cheek. "Let me check on Mom and then if you can't sleep we can sit in the den and watch a movie."

Liking that idea, she nodded. "That would be great."

He squeezed her shoulder before heading back downstairs. Anne entered her room and sank on to the bed as exhaustion settled in. "Princess?"

She'd last seen the feline scurrying under the bed when that monster had entered her room. Lifting the ruffled duster, Anne peered into the darkness. One bright eye stared back at her.

"I don't blame you, sugar. I want to hide, too."

But come tomorrow she'd be out in the open, exposed and sitting on the hot seat.

A few minutes later, Patrick appeared at the door. "A movie?"

Anything to distract herself from what lay ahead. She followed him into the den and sat beside him on the brown leather sofa across from a wide-screen Plasma television. They selected a comedy. But even before the opening credits ended, Anne's eyelids grew heavy.

Patrick slid his arm around her shoulders and drew her against him. She let her head rest against his shoulder and as sleep claimed her she thought how much she wished she'd never have to move from this spot again.

But wishes never came true.

* * *

Patrick's heart swelled with tenderness for Anne as she slept pressed against his side, the short ends of her hair tickling his chin. He'd come so close to losing her tonight. Just the memory of that knife held so closely to her graceful neck brought terror creeping up his spine. No matter what, he was not going to let anything happen to her. He'd move mountains to make sure she testified at the trial.

Part of him acknowledged that his desire to see justice done in this case wasn't totally due to Anne, but because he wished someone had come forward to testify in his father's murder. Maybe then, Patrick would find peace with his father's death.

Reverend James would say peace only came from God.

Anne had said, *All we can do is choose to love and to trust*.

He was afraid he'd never find peace, because he couldn't find love or trust inside himself.

Carlos couldn't believe it. Trinidad had screwed up. His uncle was going to be furious now. Heads would roll. Probably Carlos's first. He shuddered with dread and fear. His uncle had left him in charge and expected the pigeon's neck to be wrung before Raoul even stepped into the courtroom.

Rubbing a hand over his pock-marked face, the roughened skin scraping across his callused hand, Carlos knew there was only one way to get out of this mess. He had to take control of the situation and take the woman out before she reached New Jersey. Otherwise, he'd have to face his uncle's wrath and the prospect of Raoul revealing Carlos's secret.

Suzie, Carlos's wife, would leave him in a heartbeat if she knew he was still gambling. She'd bash his head in if she found out just how deep in debt he'd gotten himself. Carlos was only able to keep Suzie in the dark because Raoul kept the creditors at arm's length. They were probably just as scared of Raoul Domingo as Carlos was.

Because Raoul Domingo held more power than could be contained behind a set of prison bars.

Carlos made two phone calls and then left his uncle's warehouse before the sun started rising over the eastern horizon.

He was going hunting.

TWELVE

As the sun rose, Patrick woke Anne. Her sleepy eyes and messed hair were so adorable. His sister's robe engulfed Anne's slighter stature. He slipped his arm around her waist and steered her past two FBI agents to Megan's room so she could ready herself for the trial.

Careful of his wound, Patrick dressed and shaved before stepping back into the hall.

Because the two agents posted on either side of Anne's door still stood guard, he assumed that Anne had not emerged yet. With a nod, the agents acknowledged Patrick when he approached the door and softly knocked.

A moment later, the door opened and Anne stepped from the room. She was wearing the baggy brown dress suit he'd first seen her in, her brown textured purse slung over her shoulder. Her eyes were purple again, with a decidedly determined gleam. But instead of the spiky hair she had worn previously, her red hair had been blown dry and lay in feathered wisps around her face, emphasizing her delicately carved bone structure.

"Good morning," she said with a smile.

His heart rate picked up. They'd only parted for a short time, why did he feel so electrified to see her again? "You ready?" He held out his good arm for her.

"As I'll ever be," she replied and looped her arm through his.

They descended the stairs with the agents fast on their heels and found his mother sitting at the kitchen table sipping coffee. Across from her sat a man dressed in black with a white collar.

Patrick stopped short. "Reverend James?"

The reverend rose and shook Patrick's hand. "Your mother called." He smiled, the lines at the corners of his green eyes crinkling. "You must be Anne. Colleen was just telling me about you."

Anne slid her arm from Patrick and shook the reverend's offered hand. "I am."

"Colleen also tells me you are a believer."

Patrick felt his insides bunched and twisted. "We'll be leaving soon."

"There's time for Reverend James to say a blessing over Anne," Colleen said, her gaze pinning Patrick to the floor.

"I'd love that," Anne said, her gaze on Patrick.

He stared into her eyes, into her heart that was full of faith. The expectant look on her face clearly asked him to cooperate. Forcing back the bitterness that tried to rise, he inclined his head. Only for Anne would he stay.

As Reverend James prayed over Anne, Patrick couldn't stop the memories of his father's graveside service when the reverend had spoken about God's redeeming love.

Patrick had stared at the brown wooden casket, hating that his father was stuck inside that box, hating that God had allowed his father to die and hating that now Patrick had to be the "man of the house" as so many of the other mourners kept murmuring to him when they came close.

Patrick took a step back as clarity stole his breath.

He hated God for taking his father. He hated his father for taking that call. But mostly Patrick hated that he'd had to sacrifice his life for his family.

The need to bolt grabbed him by the throat. How could he have such a selfish thought? He backed up another step, needing space.

Anne glanced up, her questioning gaze trapping the breath in his lungs.

We all make choices.

But he hadn't had a choice. Had he? He'd done what was necessary. What was expected.

"Mr. McClain?"

Patrick pivoted to stare at the agent who'd stepped quietly into the kitchen. Mentally scrambling to gather his chaotic thoughts in order and show some coherency, Patrick led the officer farther down the hall. "Yes?"

"The marshals are here."

Focusing on the situation, Patrick nodded and then

moved to the trio in the kitchen. He touched Anne's elbow. "Excuse me," he said.

Reverend James raised his head with a sheepish smile. "Sorry, I tend to be verbose."

Patrick didn't comment, but he exchanged an amused glance with his mother.

"We need to leave," Patrick explained.

Colleen gave Anne a fierce hug. "You be strong."

There were tears in Anne's eyes. "I will. Thank you for everything."

"I'll see you again," Colleen assured her with a twinkle in her eye.

Anne said goodbye to the reverend then walked out the door with the agent. Patrick followed her to the big, black SUV waiting at the curb. Two men stood by the hood. As they approached, the men flashed their IDs.

"We'll be driving to the airport in Spencer and flying from there to New Jersey," the marshal named Fritz said.

"Why out of Spencer?" Patrick asked. The town was a good two-hour drive away.

"Logan's too busy. Would be too easy to take out a target in a crowd there," explained the other marshal.

"That makes sense." After last night, Patrick was glad the marshals were taking such precautions.

Fritz moved to the driver's side while the other agent, Mitchell, opened the back door for Anne. She climbed in and slid to the other side of the leather seat. Patrick made to climb in behind her but the agent held up a hand stopping him. "Sorry, sir. Only Miss Jones."

Anne scrambled to the door. "No. He's coming with us."

Frustration beat a steady rhythm at Patrick's temple as the agent adamantly shook his head. "We have our orders, miss."

"Have you talked to Lieutenant Taylor? She is expecting me to accompany Miss Jones," Patrick prodded.

"I can't let you ride with us, sir. But there's nothing I can do if you choose to follow us and purchase your own plane ticket to New Jersey," the agent said with a pointed look.

"Well enough." Patrick met Anne's nervous gaze. "I'll be right behind you all the way."

She gave him a wan smile.

The agent shut the door. She wasn't visible behind the tinted glass. Patrick waved and then headed to his car.

He was not going to let the SUV out of his sight.

Anne fiddled with the leather seam in the seat at her side as a way to keep from jumping out of the moving car. She inhaled. The SUV still had that new car smell. She wondered if she were the first to be transported in its luxury.

She glanced at the stretch of highway behind the vehicle, making sure that the little green Mini Cooper stayed within sight. She'd thought they'd lost Patrick as the agent had maneuvered his way out of the early morning commuter traffic of Boston, but every time she was on the verge of telling the driver to slow down, the Mini Cooper would pass a car and slide in behind the SUV.

The agents in the front seat didn't seem inclined to talk so Anne didn't bother. She wasn't in the mood to talk, either. They'd been driving for over an hour. The metropolitan landscape had given way to a more rural scenic drive along MA-9. Rolling hills, farms, an occasional town passed by as they zipped along.

Anne liked the name of the one they'd just passed. Cherry Hill. It sounded quaint and looked even quainter, like a good place to visit one day if she got the chance.

By the end of this day, she'd have some semblance of her life back and could return if she wanted.

A virtual hive of bees attacked her stomach at the reminder of what was coming. She should have eaten before leaving the McClains' house. She opened her purse and dug down to the bottom where she found a protein bar.

A loud pop startled Anne. She dropped the snack. The vehicle jerked and weaved. Terror streaked through her. She screamed and braced her hands against the front seat. Another loud pop. The front windshield exploded in a shower of glass.

The world spun. Anne felt a sharp pain as her head connected with the side window. The seat belt pulled painfully at her ribs, squeezing the breath from her lungs. The last thing she saw as darkness closed in was the side of the road dropping out of sight.

* * *

Patrick saw the rear tire of the SUV transporting Anne blow out. The vehicle swerved and rocked and then the windshield exploded. His heart seized momentarily in his chest, before banging against his ribs in a chaotic beat.

They'd been shot at! From where?

Patrick slammed on the brake. The little car fishtailed as the tires gripped the blacktop. Horror clogged his throat as he watched the big car in front of him spin toward a drop-off on the edge of the road.

The black car disappeared over the side. Patrick came to roaring stop, flung open the door and jumped out. He ran to the spot where the SUV went over. "Anne!"

The vehicle had landed on its top. He saw no movement from within. Patrick's world narrowed to a pinprick. Dread slammed into his heart.

He scrambled down the side of the ravine, rocks sliding beneath his feet. Heaving with shocked breaths, he slid to his knees beside the car. He checked the agents. Alive but unconscious.

Fearing what he might find, Patrick yanked on the back door, the metal groaned as he pried it open. Anne hung upside down, the seat belt holding her fast to the seat. "Anne! Oh, come on, baby, be alive." Now that he'd found he, he couldn't live without her.

He squeezed inside to check her pulse. Alive! But strapped in.

His own wound throbbed but he ignored the pain.

He could only think of her. He had to get help. He reached for his phone on his belt and let out a moan of frustration. His cell phone was on the passenger seat in his car at the top of the hill.

Helplessness, anger and panic ran a course through his system, firing off all his nerves. Grasping her by the shoulders, he gently pulled her from the wreckage.

He threw his head back and yelled toward heaven, "God, please. Help us!"

A spray of gunfire hit the dirt inches from Anne's body. Patrick threw himself over her. He had to get her away from the vehicle. If a bullet hit the engine, they'd all be dead.

A different noise drew his attention. A car screeched to a halt on the road above. Suddenly a man appeared over the rim of the hill.

Cam? His student? With a gun in his hand.

They were dead now. Patrick rose, ready to meet this threat head-on.

Cam skidded down the side of the hill. "Get back down!" He held up a shiny badge that reflected in the sunlight. Patrick squinted, not believing what he was seeing.

Patrick crouched down as relief swept through him. "You're a cop?"

"Yes, Professor." He inclined his head toward Anne. "Is she alive?"

"Unconscious. So are they." Patrick indicated the men in the front seat. "We need to get them to a hospital."

Cam nodded and pulled out a cell phone to give dispatch their location. His gaze searched the area as he squatted beside Patrick. "Did you see the assailants?"

"No. It all happened so fast. I think the shots came from that cluster of trees." Patrick pointed to a spot where a grouping of maples shaded the highway.

"I'll be back," Cam said and made his way around the SUV and toward the road.

After a long, silent stretch that pulled at Patrick's nerves, a succession of gunfire broke the air. Patrick waited, feeling vulnerable in the open.

Cam returned, his gun returned to his holster. "I took out the sniper as he was fleeing. It was Carlos Jaramillo. Domingo's nephew."

"Good. That's good." One more assassin down. How many more would they have to fight? "Who are you?"

"Cam Trang. NJPD. Lieutenant Taylor arranged for me to keep an eye on Anne." He winced, his almond-shaped eyes regretful. "I missed too many lights in town and got caught behind a slow-moving truck or I'd have been here sooner."

"Your being here wouldn't have stopped it." Anger tightened Patrick's jaw until it ached. "How could this have happened? This Carlos character was already here. Waiting."

Cam's lips twisted with frustration. "There's a leak in the system. The route the agents were given was only known by a few so it will be pretty easy to track."

Track right to Domingo, Patrick was sure.

A few minutes later, EMTs arrived along with several police and federal agents. Anne and the two marshals were put on gurneys and lifted up the hill to be put into the back of a waiting ambulance. Patrick climbed inside next to Anne. He held her hand, rubbing the skin lightly. She had to be okay. She didn't deserve this. She was just trying to do the right thing.

Lord, I don't understand. She trusts you. Is this some kind of punishment for me?

Anne would tell him God wasn't punishing him. She didn't believe that He worked that way. Patrick wasn't sure what to believe.

The ambulance took them to the nearest hospital in Harrington, just thirteen miles from Spencer, their original destination.

At the hospital Patrick paced the hall outside the room where the doctor examined Anne. Cam stood a few feet away, talking on his phone. Thankfully the federal agents had had enough clout to have Anne taken directly to a private room. Now Harrington police officers stood watch at both ends of the corridor and outside the room.

A nurse opened the door. "Mr. McClain, she's awake and asking for you."

"Thank you." Relief flooded Patrick in a rush. He entered the room. Anne lay in the bed, her eyes were open and she smiled at him. Her face sported a dark bruise over her left temple. Patrick's veins throbbed with anger at the men who did this.

The doctor, an older man with gray hair and a lean face, held a clipboard in his hands and nodded to Patrick.

Pulling a chair up to the edge of the bed, Patrick sat and took Anne's hand. He didn't know what to say so he kissed her knuckles and relished the warmth of her palm in his.

Cam stepped into the room. Anne gasped and Patrick quickly explained who Cam really was.

"Wow," she said softly. "I knew there was something up with him."

"Dr. Holt, how is her condition?" Cam asked.

"Stable. She has a slight concussion and bruised ribs from the impact."

"When can we move her?" Cam asked.

"I wouldn't recommend it for at least three days. Now if you'll excuse me I have other patients." The doctor left the room.

Anne squeezed Patrick's hand. "The trial."

Patrick nodded and addressed Cam. "Can you have the D.A. postpone the trial?"

"I was just talking with him. He'll ask the court for a postponement but is unhopeful the judge will comply because the trial was pushed forward at the request of the state."

"So what will happen if the trial isn't postponed?" Anne asked.

"The D.A. will have to make his case without your testimony."

Anne struggled to sit up. Patrick reached to help

her. She groaned and gripped his arm. "But I'm the only one who saw Domingo kill Jean Luc."

Cam nodded, his expression grim. "Yes. But there is a witness who can place him in the suite just not put the gun in his hand."

"Who?" Anne asked.

"A maid, Maria Gonzales."

"I know Maria. She's a nice woman." Anne turned her gaze to Patrick. "I have to get there. I can't let Domingo get away with murder."

"You heard the doctor. You're not in any shape to be moved for a few days," Patrick said, wanting to protect her from any more pain.

Her eyes pleaded with him. "I *have* to go."

He understood her need and admired her determination. "Cam, we're going to New Jersey."

Cam came closer, his dark eyes concerned. "Are you sure?"

Anne nodded. "Yes."

"I'll call Porter and let him know we're on our way."

"No." Patrick shook his head. "There's a leak somewhere. I'm not taking any more chances with her life. Just the three of us."

Cam considered him for a moment. "We'll have to figure a way around the agents in the hall."

"A fire alarm," Anne suggested.

Patrick glanced at her. She shrugged. "That's how I got out of detention in high school. Pulled the alarm."

"I'm afraid to ask why you had detention in the first place," Patrick said.

She grinned, a spunky light in her eyes. "Let's just say the home ec teacher ran screaming from the room and leave it at that."

He rolled his eyes. "Deal." To Cam, he said, "Do you think it will work?"

A sly gleam entered Cam's almond-shaped eyes. "We can't put other patients' lives at risk, but I can distract the agents."

"Okay, then." Patrick rubbed his hands together. "Let's make a plan."

After much talking and debating the options, they decided on a course of action. Since Anne was in a hospital gown and her own clothes were cut up from when the nurses removed them from her body, Patrick went in search of something for her to wear. Cam left to make arrangements for a plane at the airport at nearby Southbridge. Anne could only wait until the men returned, but she used the time to pray.

Patrick came back carrying a set of green scrubs.

"Where'd you find them?" she asked.

"In one of the E.R. doctor's rooms." He came to her side. "Okay, how are we going to do this?"

She held out her hand, amused by the flush of color riding up his neck. "Let me deal with this. You go see how Cam's doing."

He frowned. "Won't you need help?"

"I'll manage," she said, unwilling to have him dress her like a child. That was not the way she wanted him to view her.

"I'll be back," he stated and walked out.

"Yeah," she laughed softly. Not exactly Arnold Schwarzenegger, but he'd do. She wiggled out from beneath the sheets, gritting her teeth against the pain in her rib cage. With excruciating care, she slipped the pants on and then the top. Before tying the ends together, she touched the deep purple bruise on her chest. It could have been so much worse. "Thank you, Lord, for watching out for me."

The door opened slightly. "You okay?" Patrick called from the other side.

"Just a sec." She finished dressing. "Come in."

Patrick entered, followed by Cam. The smaller Asian man pushed a wheelchair in front of him.

"How did you get that?" she asked, as Patrick gently lifted her from the bed to set her on the seat of the wheelchair.

"I found it on the next floor down. No one will miss it for a while," Cam said. "The nurses have a shift change in about five minutes. That's when we should do this."

Patrick put his hand on her shoulder, a soothing heat spread through her at the contact. "Not too late to back out."

She covered his hand with her own. "I'm not backing out."

"All right then. Cam will distract the officers and I'll wheel you to the staff elevator, which will take us to the back parking lot. My car is right by the elevator door."

Anne took a shallow breath and still winced as she slowly let it out. "Let's do this."

THIRTEEN

As on any day in which a trial commences, the courtroom bustled with activity, much like the stage where a dramatic production was enacted. The curtain was up and the players on their marks.

It was the last day of the trial, and the prosecution's key witness wasn't coming. Her transport had been ambushed and then she skipped out on the agents assigned to guard her. District Attorney Porter had used every argument possible to delay the proceedings, but his motion for a continuance so late in the hearing was denied.

If the Boston Police could get the would-be assassin who hit the McClains the night before to turn on his boss, they could add attempted murder to Domingo's charges.

Domingo's lawyer's motions for dismissal were also denied.

Porter would have to be satisfied with the little solid evidence they had and the unsubstantiated testimony of Maria Gonzales.

Lidia sat on the bench behind the prosecutor's table where District Attorney Porter and one of his assistants were preparing for their closing remarks.

Across the aisle, Domingo sat beside his shark of an attorney, Evelyn Stein. The smug expression on his beefy face grated on Lidia's nerves. The man was going to get away with murder. It just wasn't right.

Lidia burned with anger. Someone had given the secure route the marshals were using to Domingo's men. Thankfully Anne lived, but she wouldn't be coming to testify. She could only pray Anne was safe.

Lidia leaned forward and touched Porter's shoulder. He shifted to look at her, his jaw set and his eyes grim. "You're doing great," she told him.

His expression softened. "Thanks. I'm glad you stayed."

After she'd given her testimony, she hadn't left as she usually would. Right now, her other cases would have to wait. She was here for Porter. She squeezed his shoulder and sat back. Making her support obvious was a big step. She wasn't sure where the relationship would lead, but for now she was where she was needed and that felt good.

A commotion at the back of the courtroom drew her attention along with everyone else's. The judge banged his gavel. Court security placed their hands on their sidearms.

Lidia jerked to her feet in stunned surprise as Professor McClain wheeled in Anne Jones. Lidia's heart contracted at the sight of the ugly bruise on Anne's delicate, young face. She wore scrubs and no shoes.

Porter jumped to take advantage of Anne's arrival. "Your Honor, we'd like to call our last witness to the stand."

Evelyn rose, her strident voice ringing off the walls. "I object, your honor!" Beside her, Domingo's agitation was palpable.

Judge Turner narrowed his eyes. "On what grounds?"

"Prejudicial."

Irritation etched lines around the judge's mouth. "Overruled."

"I demand a recess," Evelyn bit out.

"You demand a recess?" Judge Turner's bushy gray eyebrows rose nearly to his hairline. "Not in my courtroom, you don't, Ms. Stein."

"May we approach the bench, your honor?" Evelyn asked, her voice modulated.

With a quick flick of his wrist, the judge motioned the lawyers forward.

Lidia took advantage of the moment to go to Anne's side and gave her a gentle hug. "What are you doing here? We were told you wouldn't be able to leave the hospital for a few days and then that you slipped away from your guards."

Anne glanced up at the professor. "We thought it best not to let anyone know I was coming."

"Good thinking." Anger burned in Lidia's gut. Someone with trusted information had betrayed the justice system. She fully intended to capture their mole.

Lidia's attention strayed to the animated conversation taking place at the front of the courtroom. Looked like Ms. Stein wasn't thrilled the key witness had shown up after all. Then Lidia's gaze shifted to where Domingo sat, his dark eyes trained intimidatingly on Anne.

Lidia instinctively moved to block Domingo's view. The worm's evil had touched Anne enough already.

After a moment, the two lawyers returned to their respective tables. The judge said, "Call your last witness, Mr. Porter."

"Here we go," Anne murmured, her hand shaky as she placed it over her heart as if to calm the organ down.

"You'll be fine," Lidia assured her as she and Patrick stepped aside so that a deputy could take control of the wheelchair.

Anne was wheeled to the front of the room and sworn in. Lidia resumed her seat and Patrick sat beside her. He never took his earnest gaze off Anne.

Lidia leaned over and whispered, "You love her, don't you?"

He started. A moment passed before he answered, as if he were searching his heart. "Yes. I do."

Regret and empathy settled in Lidia's chest. "Thought so."

She had a feeling that the professor and Anne hadn't contemplated their future after the trial. Anne's only safeguard would be to reenter WITSEC. Lidia wondered how deeply the professor's feelings went.

They'd have to run very deep for him to give up everything to follow Anne.

And if not, Anne was in for a lot more heartache.

Reconvening two hours later, Judge Turner addressed the jury from his massive chair behind the tall oak bench. "Jury, have you reached a verdict?"

A man, who represented the other eleven jurors, rose. "In the case against Raoul Domingo in the murder of Jean Luc Versailles, we the jury find the defendant guilty of murder in the first degree."

From her place near the back of the courtroom, Anne closed her eyes with relief. The trial was over, finally. Domingo could appeal, but at least for now, there would be justice for Jean Luc. Domingo would go to jail and Anne could resume her life.

Her heart had been beating a steady gallop since the moment she'd first entered the courtroom and thumped against her rib cage so hard during her testimony she was surprised no one heard it through the microphone that had been placed beside her.

She hadn't wanted to look at the man who'd murdered Jean Luc, was afraid she'd falter in her statement. But one look at Patrick and his faith in her had given her the strength to face Domingo as she related how she'd seen him pull the trigger of the fatal shot that killed her employer.

And now that the verdict had been handed down, she turned her gaze on to the convicted murderer who swore at his attorney as two uniformed officers struggled to restrain him. Domingo lifted his gaze and searched the crowd until he spied Anne. A shiver slithered down her spine as those black eyes narrowed.

"You're dead!" Domingo shouted. "Don't ever think I'll forget!"

Patrick stepped in front of Anne, blocking her view. "Don't listen to him. He's going to jail for the rest of his life." Patrick reached for the handles of the chair. "Let's get out of here."

She didn't protest as he pushed the chair out into the corridor. The marble floors gleamed and the wood paneling shined. High arched windows let in light and warmth from the summer sun, yet Anne felt chilled. Domingo's threat rang in her ears. Would she ever feel safe again?

"Miss Jones?"

A man in his mid-fifties wearing a red tie, white shirt beneath a navy suit, which attractively framed his square build, approached.

"Special Agent Lofland," Anne acknowledged him.

"We need to talk," he said. "Professor, would you please join us." Lofland indicated for them to follow him through the marbled foyer of the courthouse. He headed toward a set of doors.

Patrick pushed the wheelchair, his expression grim. What was he thinking? Did he sense the lingering danger? Would he want to continue to protect her? Would he be glad to see their association end or would he want, as she did, to see where their relationship could go? He was so good at hiding his thoughts, his hurts. Anne's heart ached.

Behind them the courtroom doors burst open and the D.A. came out, mobbed by reporters.

"There's Miss Jones!" Someone cried out. The flock of reporters veered away from the D.A.

"This way. Hurry," urged Lofland as he ushered them through a door into another corridor. Behind them the door shut and locked automatically. The gaggle of voices and even pounding on the door faded as Patrick wheeled Anne into a yet another room. An interrogation room. The unadorned white walls, tiled floor and metal table with several chairs unnerved Anne.

"Professor, would you take a seat, please," Lofland asked as he pulled up a chair to face Anne.

"What's going on?" she asked, her voice shaking slightly.

"The trial may be over, but not the danger to your life," he said, his intense eyes showing compassion.

"He was convicted," Patrick stated, his brown eyes dark with concern. "Domingo will be in jail. It's not like he's part of the Italian mafia."

Lofland inclined his head. "True. But Raoul Domingo still has a powerful network and men that are loyal to him."

Anne tried to quell the rush of dread and fear flooding her system. "So what are you saying?"

"The only way the government can guarantee your continued safety is if you reenter the WITSEC program."

Anne swallowed. "And if I don't?"

"You, and anyone—" Lofland turned his gaze meaningfully onto Patrick "—you associate with will be in danger."

Anne's shoulders slumped. She had feared as much but had hoped, prayed it wouldn't be so. She glanced at Patrick. Her heart pounded. He looked stricken.

Patrick rose. "Can't you break up his 'network'?" He started to pace. "Surely there's some other way."

"There isn't. And we are working to break up his operation but it takes time. Time that Miss Jones can't afford to remain in the open," Lofland said.

A future with Patrick wasn't a possibility. She'd put him in enough danger. Had put his family in enough danger. She'd couldn't do it any longer. She resigned herself to a life, alone and in hiding. "How soon must I leave?" Anne asked.

"Now." Lofland eyed Anne and then Patrick with a speculative gleam. "We could arrange for you both to go."

Patrick stilled, his expression arrested in surprise. "Both?"

"If you want. But you'll have to leave everything behind and won't be able to contact anyone from your former life."

Anne's heart twisted as she watched the agent's words sink in him. Patrick's gaze met hers. She finally knew what he was thinking. His family was everything to him. His life too full to give up for her.

She knew he cared. She wasn't an idiot. No man would protect her the way he had if he didn't care. But he didn't love her. She was just a responsibility that he should now be free of.

Thankfully she hadn't told him her feelings. He never needed to know that she'd fallen in love with him. She raised her chin. "No. Patrick won't be coming. Just me." She gazed at Patrick. "Do you think your mother would take care of Princess?"

He blinked. "Of course. But you can't—"

She held up her hand to stop him. "I'm looking forward to starting over again. Maybe a brunette this time with green eyes," she said, forcing herself to sound upbeat.

"Anne," Patrick said softly, his voice full of pain.

"Don't. I'm going to be okay. I made a choice when I decided to testify. I knew there'd be sacrifices. How many people get to have a clean slate and a chance to reinvent themselves? Life's an adventure. I'm looking forward to it." Her voice cracked on the last word. She turned her gaze quickly back to the agent so Patrick wouldn't see the tears in her eyes. "Can I say goodbye to Lieutenant Taylor before I leave?"

"I'll have her sent in." Lofland stood. "I'll give you two a few moments."

Anne wanted to protest. She didn't want to have to say goodbye to Patrick but she stiffened her resolve and forced a smile.

As soon as the door closed behind Lofland, she said, "Thank you, Patrick, for all you've done. I couldn't have made it on my own."

He sat and pulled the wheelchair close, taking her

hands. "I wish things could be different. I wish I was free to go with you, but I'm not. I can't leave my family and you can't stay."

Her heart fragmented into a jigsaw of pieces with sharp edges that cut and wounded her from the inside out. Agony surged, but she held it back. She couldn't let him see her pain. She needed to let him go without making him feel guilt for unintentionally hurting her.

"I'm not asking you to come with me," Anne stated firmly. "Whatever we feel for each was born out of a crisis situation. It would never last for us." If she told herself that enough, maybe one day she'd actually believe it. But her heart knew the truth. He was the only man she'd ever truly love. "But, please, promise me you'll consider sending your book into a publisher or an agent."

Sadness entered his gaze. He touched her cheek. "I'll miss you."

Gut-wrenching pain blasted through her middle. She pressed into his palm. "You'll forget all about me."

"I'll never forget you," he vowed and titled her face up so that their gazes met. "Never, Anne Jones."

He didn't care about her enough to sacrifice for her. Could she blame him? She'd brought nothing but trouble to his doorstep. "Anne Jones doesn't exist anymore," she whispered.

"She'll always exist in my heart," he countered and leaned forward to capture her lips.

She kissed him back with all the love in her heart.

Love that she would never voice. Sweet torture. Blessed pain.

She pulled away, her breathing nothing more than ragged gasps. "Goodbye, Patrick."

He looked as if he wanted to say something. But, she closed her eyes and turned her head away, cutting him off before he could speak. "Please, go now."

As if on cue, the door to the room opened and Lidia stepped in, her face animated with excitement. "We found the leak. District Attorney Porter's secretary, of all people."

"That's good to know," Patrick said, his voice flat. He rose from the chair, his back straight and his eyes desolate. He nodded to Lidia and left without looking back.

"Oh, honey." Lidia gathered her into her arms. Anne let loose the aguish filling her soul.

And knew she would never be the same.

FOURTEEN

Three Months Later

"You're out here moping again?"

Patrick slanted his brother, Brody, a quelling glance. He might be outside in his mother's garden and he might be sitting with Princess on his lap while he contemplated the stars, but he was not moping. "You don't know what you're talking about."

Brody stepped in front of him, his sheriff's uniform retired for the night and in its place, he wore faded jeans and a Boston Red Sox T-shirt. His dark hair curled at the ends as it always had as a kid. "Ha! Mom says you've been moping for months. Ever since you let Anne go."

Patrick tightened his jaw. He'd had to let Anne go. Asking her to stay would have put her life in danger. "Leave me alone."

Brody's expression turned serious. He put a hand on Patrick's shoulder. "That's the problem, bro. You *are* alone and have been for too long."

"What? You aren't making sense." He shrugged off Brody's hand. "Shouldn't you be inside with Kate?"

"She and Mom went baby-stuff shopping. That'll take a while." Brody sighed as he sat next to Patrick on the bench beneath the arbor. "Let me give you some unsolicited advice."

"You do know the definition of unsolicited, don't you?" Patrick didn't wait for a response. "Unasked for and unwanted."

Brody chuckled. "Yep. Exactly. You, big brother, are so smart you're dense."

Patrick rolled his eyes. "What does that mean?"

For a moment Brody remained silent. Patrick hoped that was the end of his brother's chatter.

"Patrick, you need to let go."

Turning to face Brody, Patrick asked, "Let go? Of what?"

Brody's solemn dark eyes filled with determination and concern. "You stepped in when Dad died and we all appreciate it. We all love you. And we want you to know that your job is done. We no longer need you to be a father to us. We need you to be our brother."

Everything he'd been for the past fifteen years rebelled at the notion. "Were you elected as the spokesperson?" Patrick groused.

"Yes. And, dude, you need to get a life."

The ground beneath Patrick's feet seemed to shift, making him feel off balance. "That's easy for you to say. You left. You have Kate."

Brody's left eyebrow rose a fraction. "I left because

it was too painful here. I have Kate because God intervened in my life."

Patrick scoffed. "Now you sound like Anne."

Brody touched Patrick's shoulder again. "Until you let go of your hate and anger toward God, you're never going to be free. You're going to be stuck in this role you've saddled yourself with and always be alone."

Patrick's gut clenched. He set Princess on the ground and then stood, hoping to ease the pain rolling through him. He didn't want to hear his brother's words. Didn't want to acknowledge the truth squeezing his heart. "Have you forgiven God?"

Brody leaned his elbows on his knees. "Yes. I have. Kate has helped me understand that no matter what our circumstances, God is always God. He doesn't change. I'm not saying it's easy. But the hate and anger can eat your soul if you're not careful."

That was true. Patrick could feel the darkness chomping through him. He hadn't been aware of it until Anne had whirled into his life. And now hearing Brody confirming the knowledge made his heart race with possibilities. "But what about Mom?"

Brody stood, his expression patient. "Mom's okay. She's been waiting for you to move on so that she could."

Patrick paced the patio as he worked through the concept. He thought he'd been doing the right thing by always being here for his mother. Always being available for his siblings. *We no longer need you to be a father to us. We need you to be our brother.*

We all make choices, Anne had said. Patrick had chosen the role he'd thought necessary when he was a teen. But now? Now he needed to choose a different path.

Patrick stared up at the stars, seeing the twinkling lights through a blur that wouldn't be wiped away by cleaning his glasses. For the past few months he'd been miserable and missed Anne so much there were times when it was a physical ache in his chest.

Let go of your hate and anger toward God.

A sensation of fullness grew inside of him, a deep rising of emotion that clogged his throat and pushed at his lungs.

Brody slipped an arm around his shoulders. Patrick moaned as the tears he'd never shed for the loss of his father burst out. He cried in his brother's arms as the grief that had been buried beneath the hurt and betrayal for so many years gushed out.

All we can do is choose to love and to trust.

As the tears subsided and a calmness he'd never experienced before settled in, Patrick lifted up a prayer asking God to give him another chance.

Now all he had left was the impossible task of finding Anne.

Lidia hated the paperwork part of her job. Filling in forms, making sure all the t's were crossed and the i's dotted wasn't just a cliché, it was a reality she knew could make or break the case when presented in a courtroom.

Today she was putting the finishing details to the report of a burglary/homicide at a convenience store on the strip. Summers were always bad with the teenagers out of school, bored and looking for a thrill. She would be glad when the schools opened again in a few weeks.

"Hey, Taylor!"

Lidia sighed at the all-too-familiar desk sergeant's bellow. Morales never just picked up the phone to buzz her. No, he had to yell through the station house like he was calling some errant child on the playground. She got up and stretched her back before heading in the direction of the sergeant's desk.

"Got a live one for you," the sergeant joked, his craggy face breaking into a grin.

Morales liked his joke. The joke was getting old.

Lidia followed the direction of the sergeant's pointed finger. She blinked and then moved forward. "Professor?"

Professor McClain met her, his hand outstretched, his gaze determined and desperate. "Lieutenant. Thank you for seeing me."

"What are you doing in New Jersey?"

"Is there somewhere private we could talk?"

"Sure." She led him down a hall to an interrogation room. Once inside, she leaned against the wall, curiosity eating away at her patience. "What's up, Professor?"

"I have to find Anne. I should never have let her go. I'm miserable without her. Agent Lofland won't help. You're my only hope."

Stunned didn't describe the reaction running

through Lidia. A bit of anger, a bit of joy and a huge dose of protectiveness for Anne made Lidia's gaze narrow. "She was pretty broken up when you left her."

He scrubbed a hand over his face. "I know. I made an enormous mistake. I'm willing to do whatever it takes to be with her. I just have to find her."

If his expression wasn't so sincere and his eyes so beseeching, Lidia would have dismissed him off the bat. But compassion and the need to see love triumph compelled her to say, "I don't know if I can help you but I'll see what I can do."

Patrick sat at his desk in his office, his hand placed atop the pages of his manuscript. A cover letter addressed to a literary agent waited for Patrick's signature. An addressed envelope sat off to the side. He just lacked the courage to go through with it.

He was trying hard to let go of the role he'd had for so long and step out of the comfort zone he'd lived within.

His first step had been to resume going to church. The church that Anne had introduced him to. When he sat in the pew near the front he could almost imagine her sitting there beside him. He was learning about God, slowly coming to terms with his father's death.

His second step had been to tell his family about his book. They'd been excited and encouraging.

He was still hopeful that his third step would one day come to fruition. But as yet he'd been unsuccessful in locating Anne. He stopped by the federal building every other day to ask Agent Lofland for help.

And every time he was told the same thing—that her whereabouts were confidential. Patrick had hoped that Lieutenant Taylor would be able to help, but it had been three weeks and no word.

Today he was determined to mail off his manuscript.

His desk phone rang. Glad for the distraction he answered, expecting Sharon, but was surprised to hear Lieutenant Taylor.

"Professor, I think you need a vacation."

His heart jumped. "A vacation? Where?"

"I hear Disney World is a fun place."

Hope rose, making his palms sweat. "Okay. I could do Disney World."

"Mondays seem to be a less crowded day. And at two in the afternoon Cinderella's Golden Carousel is a must."

"Thank you for that tip."

"You're welcome. And, Professor?"

"Yes?"

"God bless you."

Patrick checked his watch. Five minutes to two. He stood in front of the beautifully ornate Golden Carousel. The lilting music played and children laughed, filling the air with the delighted sounds of the happiest place on earth—Disney World.

Patrick wasn't sure what he was supposed to be

looking for. His nerves were stretched tight as he searched the crowd, looking for Anne.

Would she still have the spiky red hair or would she have changed? Would she have purple or blue eyes? Would he ever be able to find her in the crowd of determined and pleased park-goers?

The Florida sun beat down on his head, so welcome from the cold that had breezed into Boston the past week.

Maybe he was on the wrong side of the carousel? He walked in a clockwise direction, his gaze scanning the carousel, the line, the other rides. When he was back to where he started he checked his watch again. Ten minutes after.

His spirit plummeted. He was never going to find her. He moved to sit on a bench that faced the carousel. He'd wait all day if that's what it took. He wasn't going to give up now.

A family with a toddler and a girl of about six stopped close by.

"Mommy, look. There she is," exclaimed the little girl and pointed toward one of the many female Disney characters. The family walked off toward a ride.

A character, Geppetto, Patrick was pretty sure, strolled past.

Patrick's gaze searched the crowd. But how on earth would he ever recognize her?

"Patrick?"

The voice so familiar came from his right.

He sprang to his feet, his gaze swinging to the

woman who stood a short distance away. For a moment he was stunned speechless, then his heart leaped and joy washed over him as he took in the short dark hair with a red bow, that framed wide green eyes and ruby-red lips. The blue and yellow dress hugged curves he'd been dreaming about.

"Snow White," he stated in stunned disbelief.

"Follow me." She gestured to him with a white gloved hand.

Keeping a discreet distance, he followed her as she led him toward the ride named after her character. She lingered a moment near the entrance to greet the many children and adults who wanted to hug Snow White. Then she glanced at him, again motioned for him to follow.

Patrick hurried to catch up as she rounded the corner of the building. When he came around the corner she was nowhere to be seen.

But then he noticed an open doorway. He stepped through into an orange colored hallway with exposed pipes.

And she was there waiting for him.

"What are you doing here, Patrick?"

Wanting nothing more than to take her into his arms, he forced himself to remain still. He had a hurdle to cross first. "I want to ask for your forgiveness and if I can have a second chance."

Her hand went to her heart. "Nothing's changed."

He stepped forward and gathered her hand in his. "I've changed, but my love for you hasn't."

The adorably stunned expression on her face tugged at his heart. "Yes, I love you," he repeated.

"But your family. Your career," she protested, her eyes growing watery.

"They understand. There are universities in Florida, too. But the real question is, do you love me?"

A tear crested her lashes and fell. "Yes," she whispered. "Oh, yes."

His heart soared. "Then nothing else matters. You are my priority. As long as we're together. We'll work things out."

A smile of pure joy lit her face. She threw her arms around his neck. "I'm so happy to see you. I've been praying that God would bring us back together."

Patrick pressed his lips to her mouth and said, "He's answered both of our prayers."

EPILOGUE

Lidia fiddled with the buttons of her long, leather jacket and struggled to resist the urge to check her lipstick as she waited outside the courthouse for District Attorney Porter. Few clouds dotted the clear September sky and the fall leaves were beginning to turn. She pulled the corner of her collar closer against the crisp bite to the air that announced the coming change in the weather.

She leaned against a stone pillar, hoping to avoid the notice of the circling media and other bystanders waiting for the D.A. to emerge after prosecuting a gruesome murder case against a renowned psychologist. Lidia had no doubt the sicko-pycho would be found guilty; she'd led the investigation and it was airtight. And with Porter's amazing skill as a prosecutor, the guy would be put away for life.

The doors to the courthouse opened. The defense attorney, a polished, younger up-and-coming man with political ambitions, came out and was immediately descended upon by the reporters. From where Lidia stood she couldn't hear the lawyer's statement, but she could guess he was dissing the justice system and probably purporting his client's innocence.

Her gaze shifted back to the open door as Porter came outside. A smile tugged at her heart as well as her mouth. She loved to watch him in action. Cool, calm and full of honor. Not only was Christopher Porter turning out to be a considerate and attentive companion, but she respected and admired his prowess in the court.

The man had stolen her heart.

As he threaded his way through the jumble of media who'd also caught sight of him, his gaze searched for someone. She waved. His expression softened. And her smile widened. He'd been looking for her. He pushed his way through the crowd toward Lidia.

As he approached, she stepped away from the pillar and headed to her cruiser parked at the curb. Pretending to be his escort had served them well as both a means to keep the media from sniffing out the truth of their relationship, and also to show the NJPD's support of the district attorney.

Once they were secure inside the vehicle and on their way, Lidia asked, "How did it go?"

"Well. It's a solid case, thanks to you and your team. We reconvene in the morning for closing arguments."

"That creep should get the death penalty." She thought of the victim, a twenty-year-old college student who'd come to the doctor for help, only to end up dismembered and dumped in the ocean.

"Agreed."

Mentally shaking off the image of the victim, she said, "On a better note, Domingo's dead."

Porter lifted an eyebrow. "Really? Details."

Lidia grinned at his use of her phrase. "A shank to the kidneys. He bled out before the guards could get to him."

"Can't say that I'm sad."

"No. You reap what you sow in life. He may have held a lot of power on the outside, but, apparently, not on the inside."

"You do know what this means, don't you?"

"Of course I do." Giddy anticipation bubbled through her.

"Then let's go see Lofland."

"My thought exactly," she stated as she headed the car toward the Federal Building. "Anne and the professor can come out of hiding."

She couldn't wait to tell them.

Patrick entered the two-story town house he shared with his wife, Anne. Around him splashes of color permeated every inch of space. But it wasn't a chaotic collection of hues and tones but a blending of personalities and styles. Brown and beiges, leather and stone for him with complementing accents of plush fabrics in shades of red, purple and green for her.

The aroma of warm bread and roasting meat tantalized his hunger. "Hello?"

"In here," Anne called from the kitchen.

He couldn't wait to see her. Every day when he came home from the University of Florida, where he taught freshman economics under the name Professor Kelley—having taken his mother's maiden name—Patrick held his breath, praying that today wasn't the day their whereabouts had been compromised. The fear bordered on fanatical but there was a real threat that one day someone would find him or Anne and their lives would be shattered.

He entered the kitchen and took a moment to stare at his wife. Her darkened hair had grown to touch her shoulders and accentuated her creamy skin. She wore a loose ruffled blouse and shorts. Her pink-tipped toes were bare. Every day she grew more beautiful and more precious to him. The sacrifices of walking away from his career and his family had been well worth her love.

She turned her blue-eyed gaze toward him, her eyes shining with happiness. She'd gotten in the habit of taking the green contacts out at home. "How was your day?"

He rolled up the sleeve of his oxford button-down shirt. "Good. Glad to be home. My stomach wants to know what's for dinner."

"A celebratory meal," she announced. "Pot roast, potatoes, carrots and French bread."

He slid his arms around her waist and pulled her close. "What are we celebrating?"

"I received my first A today in my English class."

She had enrolled at the university as a freshman. A big step. But as yet hadn't picked a major.

"That does deserve celebrating," he said and bent to capture her lips as pride for her swelled inside his chest.

A knock at the front door startled them apart.

"Are you expecting someone?" he asked.

Anne shook her head, her eyes wide. "Could be the neighbor," she said, but her voice lacked conviction.

Patrick hated the awful feeling of uncertainty that around any corner, at any knock, their lives could be torn apart by a vengeful madman. "Stay here," he said and went to the door.

Peering through the peephole, he caught his breath. He took a step back. His heart hammered against his ribs. Anxiety twisted his gut.

"Who's there?" Anne whispered to him as she came to his side and slipped her hand into his.

"Lieutenant Taylor and District Attorney Porter," he replied. What could their appearance on his and Anne's doorstep mean?

Anne quickly unlocked the door and yanked it open. With a squeal of delight she flung her arms around Lieutenant Taylor. "Oh, my word," Anne exclaimed in a rush of words. "What are you doing here? Come in. I'm so happy to see you."

His wife obviously had a different reaction.

The officer laughed and hugged Anne back, then allowed herself to be dragged inside.

Porter followed at a more sedate pace. "Professor."

They shook hands, but Patrick's voice deserted him. He closed and locked the door behind their guests.

"We have news," Porter stated, his lined face relaxed, not at all grim or concerned.

That was a good sign, wasn't it? "Please, sit," Patrick invited.

When they were seated, Taylor and Anne on the couch, Porter on the love seat and Patrick in the side chair, Patrick asked, "What news do you bring?"

"Domingo is dead," Lieutenant Taylor announced.

An oppressive stone of dread that constantly rode Patrick's back lifted. He nearly slid off the chair.

"Does that mean—" Anne blinked as tears filled her eyes. "We don't have to hide anymore?"

"That's right. The New Jersey police have worked diligently to break up what was left of his network. The threat to your life died with Domingo," Porter explained, his voice light.

Anne held out her hand to Patrick. He clasped her delicate fingers within his, feeling the slim wedding band that matched the one on his finger. He knew exactly what he wanted to do. He wanted to give Anne the wedding she deserved, in a church with family and friends around. The little ceremony in Vegas over the Fourth of the July had been nice and corny and wonderful, but now they were free to live. Really live.

He pulled Anne to her feet so they stood facing each other. He stared deep into her eyes, seeing himself reflected in the crystal-blue depths. "Anne, will you marry me again? This time in Boston?" he asked, totally unconcerned that they had an audience. "With our family and friends as witnesses."

Her smile outshined the sun. "Yes. Oh, yes."

* * * * *

Be sure to read
DOUBLE CROSS,
Terri Reed's next book in
THE McCLAINS *miniseries.*
Available September 2008
from Love Inspired Suspense.

Dear Reader,

I hope you enjoyed the journey that Anne and Patrick made through this book. Anne had a tough choice to make, one I hope that I would have the courage to make if I were put into her shoes.

Though at first her faith was tentative at best, Anne allowed God to work in her life and she was able to help Patrick see that God loved him, even though he felt betrayed by God. Patrick's unresolved grief tainted his view of himself and his life, thus causing him to close off his heart to love.

I think too often people, Christians especially, fall prey to the fallacy that having faith will guarantee a smooth sailing life without any heartache. And when trouble comes, as it inevitably does, we're quick to blame God rather than turn to Him for comfort. God's word is clear that trials will be a part of our lives, but through those trials, we have the opportunity to grow in our faith. I pray that as you and I face difficulties we will look to God for comfort, peace and guidance.

May God bless you always,

QUESTIONS FOR DISCUSSION

1. What made you pick up this book to read? Did it live up to your expectations?

2. Did you think Anne and Patrick were realistic characters? Did their romance build believably?

3. If you were faced with the choices that Anne had, how do you think you'd respond?

4. How much of Anne's background shaped who she was? How much of your background shapes who you are?

5. Talk about a time in your life when you were faced with a difficult choice. How did your faith help you through this?

6. Patrick hadn't grieved for his father's death as a boy. How did this affect his life?

7. Is there something in your life that you haven't grieved that is affecting your faith?

8. Patrick thought he had to fulfill a certain role in his family: how did this affect his life? Is there a role you have in your family? How does this affect your life? For Patrick, his role needed to change

so that he could find happiness. How can your role change to make your life more enjoyable?

9. Did you notice the scripture in the beginning of the book? What application does it have to your life?

10. Did the author's use of language/writing style make this an enjoyable read? Would you read more from this author?

11. What will be your most vivid memories of this book?

12. What overarching lessons about life, love and faith did you learn from this story?

Love Inspired
SUSPENSE
RIVETING INSPIRATIONAL ROMANCE

Near her isolated mountain cabin, Martha Gabler
encounters a handsome stranger who claims he's an ATF
agent working undercover. Furthermore, Tristan Sinclair
says that if she doesn't play along as his girlfriend, they'll
both end up dead. So Martha calls up all her faith and
turns her trust to Tristan....

Look for
The
GUARDIAN'S
MISSION
by Shirlee McCoy

Steeple
Hill®

Available August wherever books are sold.

Love Inspired
HISTORICAL
INSPIRATIONAL HISTORICAL ROMANCE

Cowboy Kody Douglas is a half breed, a man of two worlds who is at home in neither. When he stumbles upon Charlotte Porter's South Dakota farmhouse and finds her abandoned, he knows he can't leave her alone. Will these two outcasts find love and comfort together in a world they once thought cold and heartless?

Look for

The Journey Home
by
LINDA FORD

*Available August 2008
wherever books are sold.*

www.SteepleHill.com

REQUEST YOUR FREE BOOKS!
2 FREE RIVETING INSPIRATIONAL NOVELS
PLUS 2 FREE MYSTERY GIFTS

Love Inspired. SUSPENSE

YES! Please send me 2 FREE Love Inspired® Suspense novels and my 2 FREE mystery gifts (gifts are worth about $10). After receiving them, if I don't wish to receive any more books, I can return the shipping statement marked "cancel". If I don't cancel, I will receive 4 brand-new novels every month and be billed just $4.24 per book in the U.S. or $4.74 per book in Canada, plus 25¢ shipping and handling per book and applicable taxes, if any*. That's a savings of over 20% off the cover price! I understand that accepting the 2 free books and gifts places me under no obligation to buy anything. I can always return a shipment and cancel at any time. Even if I never buy another book, the two free books and gifts are mine to keep forever.

123 IDN ERXX   323 IDN ERXM

Name	(PLEASE PRINT)	
Address		Apt. #
City	State/Prov.	Zip/Postal Code

Signature (if under 18, a parent or guardian must sign)

Order online at www.LoveInspiredSuspense.com
Or mail to Steeple Hill Reader Service:
IN U.S.A.: P.O. Box 1867, Buffalo, NY 14240-1867
IN CANADA: P.O. Box 609, Fort Erie, Ontario L2A 5X3

Not valid to current subscribers of Love Inspired Suspense books.

Want to try two free books from another series?
Call 1-800-873-8635 or visit www.morefreebooks.com

* Terms and prices subject to change without notice. N.Y. residents add applicable sales tax. Canadian residents will be charged applicable provincial taxes and GST. Offer not valid in Quebec. This offer is limited to one order per household. All orders subject to approval. Credit or debit balances in a customer's account(s) may be offset by any other outstanding balance owed by or to the customer. Please allow 4 to 6 weeks for delivery. Offer available while quantities last.

Your Privacy: Steeple Hill Books is committed to protecting your privacy. Our Privacy Policy is available online at www.SteepleHill.com or upon request from the Reader Service. From time to time we make our lists of customers available to reputable third parties who may have a product or service of interest to you. If you would prefer we not share your name and address, please check here. ☐

LISUS08R

Love Inspired
SUSPENSE

TITLES AVAILABLE NEXT MONTH

Don't miss these four stories in August

THE GUARDIAN'S MISSION by Shirlee McCoy
The Sinclair Brothers
Heartbroken after a failed engagement, Martha Gabler
heads to her family's cabin for some time alone. But her
retreat soon turns deadly. With gunrunners threatening
her life, Martha has to trust undercover ATF agent
Tristan Sinclair to protect her—and heal her heart.

HIDDEN DECEPTION by Leann Harris
Elena Segura Jackson is frightened when she stumbles
upon her employee murdered, and she's terrified when
the killer starts vandalizing her shop. Clearly, she has
something the killer wants...but what is it? With Detective
Daniel Stillwater's help, can she find it in time to save
her life?

HER ONLY PROTECTOR by Lisa Mondello
All bounty hunter Gil Waite wants is to find a fugitive and
collect the reward. Then he meets the fugitive's beautiful
sister. Trapped in Colombia while rescuing her brother's
baby, Sonia Montgomery needs Gil on her side if she's ever
going to get herself and her niece safely home.

RIVER OF SECRETS by Lynette Eason
Amy Graham fled to Brazil to atone for her family's sins—
she never expected to discover Micah McKnight, the man
her mother betrayed. Micah doesn't remember who he is,
and Amy is too scared to tell him...but as danger escalates,
Amy's secrets could cost her everything.

LISCNM0708